U0108759

The Elements of Style
寫作風格之要素

William Strunk Jr.
威廉・史壯克

商務印書館

The Elements of Style 寫作風格之要素

作　　者：William Strunk Jr. 威廉・史壯克
翻　　譯：商務印書館編輯部
責任編輯：仇茵晴
封面設計：楊愛文
出　　版：商務印書館 (香港) 有限公司
香港筲箕灣耀興道 3 號東滙廣場 8 樓
http://www.commercialpress.com.hk
發　　行：香港聯合書刊物流有限公司
香港新界大埔汀麗路 36 號中華商務印刷大廈 3 字樓
印　　刷：中華商務彩色印刷有限公司
香港新界大埔汀麗路 36 號中華商務印刷大廈 14 字樓
版　　次：2019 年 6 月第 1 版第 4 次印刷
©2016 商務印書館 (香港) 有限公司
ISBN 978 962 07 0421 5
Printed in Hong Kong

版權所有　不得翻印

序一

香港學生寫作的英語總是要「深」要「長」。即是說用字要深，越是人家不懂的越好，但很多時卻未能掌握字的含意，以及引申義和聯想等，導致弄巧反拙。另外，句子要長，於是用了很多的關係代名詞（relative pronoun），例如 which 、who 、that 之類，以及關係從句（relative clause），於是句子變成像紮腳布那麼長，短則一段一句，長則連綿半頁也不了斷。又如 not only...but also 的句式結構，學生最喜歡使用，差不多每篇文章或譯文都會出現。要知句子越長，就越容易導致語法錯誤，因為有時未能兼顧前後的「一致」（agreement）。

《寫作風格之要素》中的「金句」俯拾即是，不少都打中我們寫英語的要害。例如，使用主動語態（Use the active voice）、刪去贅字（Omit needless words）、避免使用一連串結構鬆散的句子（Avoid a succession of loose sentences）等，都一語中的，非常值得我們參考。

本書在 2011 年獲選為美國時代雜誌 100 本最佳和最具影響力的英語書籍，它對寫作的裨益是有目共睹的。

恒生管理學院常務副校長
翻譯學院院長

方梓勳教授

序二

千方百計 皆在其中

工具書與經典本來南轅北轍，風馬牛不相及，但在英語寫作的範疇，有一著作既可用作工具，又可當經典奉讀。說 *The Elements of Style* 是寫作指南，等於說《紅樓夢》是本小說或莎士比亞是個作者，沒有錯，卻非常有欠準確。

The Elements of Style 令人心悅誠服，因為它躬行所言，說的一套就是做的一套，英文所謂 "practice what it preaches"。這本書不僅大談風格，更寫出了風格。幾年前，我在《EQ 一英文智商》一書提出「風格覺識」（stylistic awareness）這個概念，敦促老師和家長不管用甚麼千方百計，都要培養學生和孩子對遣詞造句與寫作風格的敏感度和認知力。今日讀到 *The Elements of Style* 的中譯本《寫作風格之要素》，赫然發現這本書就是千方百計，因為千方百計皆在其中。

嚴選工具的重要性不下於擇偶。英文有句話是這樣說的，If the only tool you have is a hammer, you tend to see every problem as a nail。意思是如果一個人只懂得用錘子，就難免會將所有要解決的問題都看成是釘子。中國人也說，工欲善其事，必先利其器。你的寫作如何，跟你的寫作工具箱裏面放了些甚麼大有關係。《寫作風格之要素》是利器，不第一時間把它放進工具箱，是你的損失。

林沛理

CONTENTS

I. Introductory *1*

II. Elementary Rules of Usage *5*

1. Form the possessive singular of nouns with 's *7*
2. In a series of three or more terms with a single conjunction, use a comma after each term except the last *8*
3. Enclose parenthetic expressions between commas *9*
4. Place a comma before *and* or *but* introducing an independent clause *12*
5. Do not join independent clauses by a comma *14*
6. Do not break sentences in two *16*
7. A participial phrase at the beginning of a sentence must refer to the grammatical subject *17*
8. Divide words at line-ends, in accordance with their formation and pronunciation *19*

III. Elementary Principles of Composition *21*

9. Make the paragraph the unit of composition: one paragraph to each topic *23*

10. As a rule, begin each paragraph with a topic sentence; end it in conformity with the beginning ... *26*

11. Use the active voice ... *31*

12. Put statements in positive form ... *34*

13. Omit needless words ... *36*

14. Avoid a succession of loose sentences ... *39*

15. Express co-ordinate ideas in similar form ... *41*

16. Keep related words together ... *44*

17. In summaries, keep to one tense ... *48*

18. Place the emphatic words of a sentence at the end ... *50*

IV. A Few Matters of Form ... *53*

V. Words and Expressions Commonly Misused ... *59*

VI. Words Often Misspelled ... *81*

I

Introductory

This book is intended for use in English courses in which the practice of composition is combined with the study of literature. It aims to give in brief space the principal requirements of plain English style. It aims to lighten the task of instructor and student by concentrating attention (in Chapters II and III) on a few essentials, the rules of usage and principles of composition most commonly violated. The numbers of the sections may be used as references in correcting manuscript.

The book covers only a small portion of the field of English style, but the experience of its writer has been that once past the essentials, students profit most by individual instruction based on the problems of their own work, and that each instructor has his own body of theory, which he prefers to that offered by any textbook.

The writer's colleagues in the Department of English in Cornell University have greatly helped him in the preparation of his manuscript. Mr. George McLane Wood has kindly consented to the inclusion under Rule 11 of some material from his *Suggestions to Authors.*

The following books are recommended for reference or further study: in connection with Chapters II and IV, F. Howard Collins, *Author and Printer* (Henry Frowde); Chicago University Press, *Manual of Style*; T. L. De Vinne, *Correct Composition* (The Century Company); Horace Hart, *Rules for Compositors and Printers* (Oxford University Press); George McLane Wood, *Extracts from the Style-Book of the Government Printing Office* (United States Geological Survey);

in connection with Chapters III and V, Sir Arthur Quiller-Couch, *The Art of Writing* (Putnams), especially the chapter, Interlude on Jargon; George McLane Wood, *Suggestions to Authors* (United States Geological Survey); John Leslie Hall, *English Usage* (Scott, Foresman and Co.); James P. Kelly, *Workmanship in Words* (Little, Brown and Co.).

It is an old observation that the best writers sometimes disregard the rules of rhetoric. When they do so, however, the reader will usually find in the sentence some compensating merit, attained at the cost of the violation. Unless he is certain of doing as well, he will probably do best to follow the rules. After he has learned, by their guidance, to write plain English adequate for everyday uses, let him look, for the secrets of style, to the study of the masters of literature.

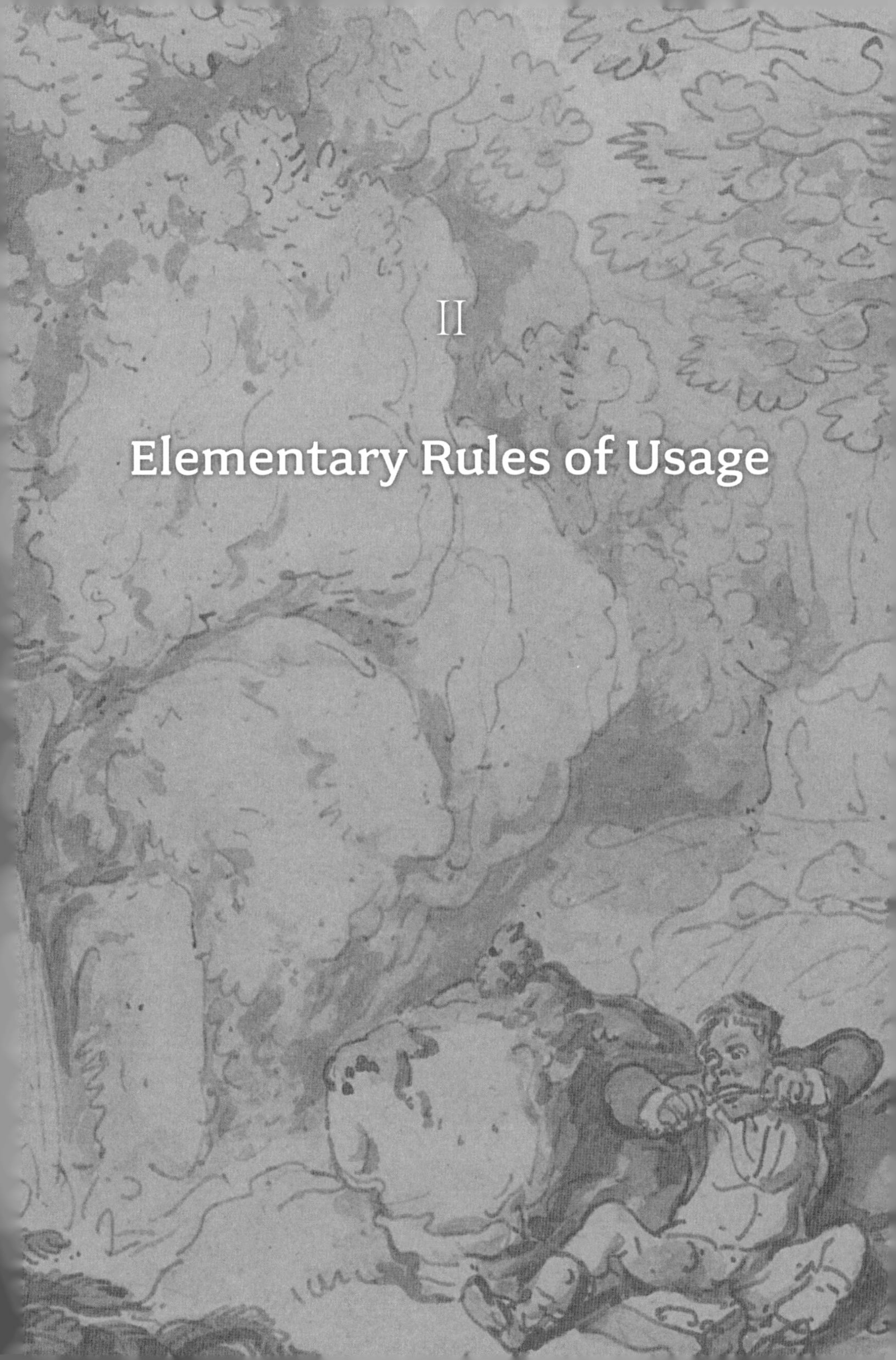

II

Elementary Rules of Usage

1. Form the possessive singular of nouns with 's

Follow this rule whatever the final consonant. Thus write,

Charles's friend

Burns's poems

the witch's malice

This is the usage of the United States Government Printing Office and of the Oxford University Press.

Exceptions are the possessives of ancient proper names in *-es* and *-is*, the possessive *Jesus'*, and such forms as *for conscience' sake*, *for righteousness' sake*. But such forms as *Achilles' heel*, *Moses' laws*, *Isis' temple* are commonly replaced by

the heel of Achilles

the laws of Moses

the temple of Isis

The pronominal possessives *hers*, *its*, *theirs*, *yours*, and *oneself* have no apostrophe.

In a series of three or more terms with a single conjunction, use a comma after each term except the last

Thus write,

> red, white, and blue
>
> honest, energetic, but headstrong
>
> He opened the letter, read it, and made a note of its contents.

This is also the usage of the Government Printing Office and of the Oxford University Press.

In the names of business firms the last comma is omitted, as

> Brown, Shipley and Company

The abbreviation *etc.*, even if only a single term comes before it, is always preceded by a comma.

3. Enclose parenthetic expressions between commas

The best way to see a country, unless you are pressed for time, is to travel on foot.

This rule is difficult to apply; it is frequently hard to decide whether a single word, such as *however*, or a brief phrase, is or is not parenthetic. If the interruption to the flow of the sentence is but slight, the writer may safely omit the commas. But whether the interruption be slight or considerable, he must never omit one comma and leave the other. Such punctuation as

Marjorie's husband, Colonel Nelson paid us a visit yesterday.

My brother you will be pleased to hear, is now in perfect health.

is indefensible.

Non-restrictive relative clauses are, in accordance with this rule, set off by commas.

The audience, which had at first been indifferent, became more and more interested.

Similar clauses introduced by *where* and *when* are similarly punctuated.

> In 1769, when Napoleon was born, Corsica had but recently been acquired by France.
>
> Nether Stowey, where Coleridge wrote *The Rime of the Ancient Mariner*, is a few miles from Bridgewater.

In these sentences the clause introduced by *which*, *when*, and *where* are non-restrictive; they do not limit the application of the words on which they depend, but add, parenthetically, statements supplementing those in the principal clauses. Each sentence is a combination of two statements which might have been made independently.

> The audience was at first indifferent. Later it became more and more interested.
>
> Napoleon was born in 1769. At that time Corsica had but recently been acquired by France.
>
> Coleridge wrote *The Rime of the Ancient Mariner* at Nether Stowey. Nether Stowey is only a few miles from Bridgewater.

Restrictive relative clauses are not set off by commas.

> The candidate who best meets these requirements will obtain the place.

In this sentence the relative clause restricts the application of the word *candidate* to a single person. Unlike those above, the sentence cannot be split into two independent statements.

The abbreviations *etc.* and *jr.* are always preceded by a comma, and except at the end of a sentence, followed by one.

Similar in principle to the enclosing of parenthetic expressions between commas is the setting off by commas of phrases or dependent clauses preceding or following the main clause of a sentence. The sentences quoted in this section and under Rules 4, 5, 6, 7, 16, and 18 should afford sufficient guidance.

If a parenthetic expression is preceded by a conjunction, place the first comma before the conjunction, not after it.

> He saw us coming, and unaware that we had learned of his treachery, greeted us with a smile.

Place a comma before *and* or *but* introducing an independent clause

The early records of the city have disappeared, and the story of its first years can no longer be reconstructed.

The situation is perilous, but there is still one chance of escape.

Sentences of this type, isolated from their context, may seem to be in need of rewriting. As they make complete sense when the comma is reached, the second clause has the appearance of an afterthought. Further, *and* is the least specific of connectives. Used between independent clauses, it indicates only that a relation exists between them without defining that relation. In the example above, the relation is that of cause and result. The two sentences might be rewritten:

As the early records of the city have disappeared, the story of its first years can no longer be reconstructed.

Although the situation is perilous, there is still one chance of escape.

Or the subordinate clauses might be replaced by phrases:

> Owing to the disappearance of the early records of the city, the story of its first years can no longer be reconstructed.
>
> In this perilous situation, there is still one chance of escape.

But a writer may err by making his sentences too uniformly compact and periodic, and an occasional loose sentence prevents the style from becoming too formal and gives the reader a certain relief. Consequently, loose sentences of the type first quoted are common in easy, unstudied writing. But a writer should be careful not to construct too many of his sentences after this pattern (see Rule 14).

Two-part sentences of which the second member is introduced by *as* (in the sense of *because*), *for*, *or*, *nor*, and *while* (in the sense of *and at the same time*) likewise require a comma before the conjunction.

If a dependent clause, or an introductory phrase requiring to be set off by a comma, precedes the second independent clause, no comma is needed after the conjunction.

> The situation is perilous, but if we are prepared to act promptly, there is still one chance of escape.

For two-part sentences connected by an adverb, see the next section.

5. Do not join independent clauses by a comma

If two or more clauses, grammatically complete and not joined by a conjunction, are to form a single compound sentence, the proper mark of punctuation is a semicolon.

> Stevenson's romances are entertaining; they are full of exciting adventures.
>
> It is nearly half past five; we cannot reach town before dark.

It is of course equally correct to write the above as two sentences each, replacing the semicolons by periods.

> Stevenson's romances are entertaining. They are full of exciting adventures.
>
> It is nearly half past five. We cannot reach town before dark.

If a conjunction is inserted, the proper mark is a comma (Rule 4).

> Stevenson's romances are entertaining, for they are full of exciting adventures.
>
> It is nearly half past five, and we cannot reach town before dark.

Note that if the second clause is preceded by an adverb, such as *accordingly*, *besides*, *so*, *then*, *therefore*, or *thus*, and not by a conjunction, the semicolon is still required.

> I had never been in the place before; so I had difficulty in finding my way about.

In general, however, it is best, in writing, to avoid using *so* in this manner; there is danger that the writer who uses it at all may use it too often. A simple correction, usually serviceable, is to omit the word *so*, and begin the first clause with *as*:

> As I had never been in the place before, I had difficulty in finding my way about.

If the clauses are very short, and are alike in form, a comma is usually permissible:

> Man proposes, God disposes.
>
> The gate swung apart, the bridge fell, the portcullis was drawn up.

6. Do not break sentences in two

In other words, do not use periods for commas.

> I met them on a Cunard liner several years ago. Coming home from Liverpool to New York.

> He was an interesting talker. A man who had traveled all over the world and lived in half a dozen countries.

In both these examples, the first period should be replaced by a comma, and the following word begun with a small letter.

It is permissible to make an emphatic word or expression serve the purpose of a sentence and to punctuate it accordingly:

> Again and again he called out. No reply.

The writer must, however, be certain that the emphasis is warranted, and that he will not be suspected of a mere blunder in punctuation.

Rules 3, 4, 5, and 6 cover the most important principles in the punctuation of ordinary sentences; they should be so thoroughly mastered that their application becomes second nature.

A participial phrase at the beginning of a sentence must refer to the grammatical subject

Walking slowly down the road, he saw a woman accompanied by two children.

The word *walking* refers to the subject of the sentence, not to the woman. If the writer wishes to make it refer to the woman, he must recast the sentence:

He saw a woman, accompanied by two children, walking slowly down the road.

Participial phrases preceded by a conjunction or by a preposition, nouns in apposition, adjectives, and adjective phrases come under the same rule if they begin the sentence.

* On arriving in Chicago, his friends met him at the station.

When he arrived (or, On his arrival) in Chicago, his friends met him at the station.

* A soldier of proved valor, they entrusted him with the defence of the city.

A soldier of proved valor, he was entrusted with the defence of the city.

* Young and inexperienced, the task seemed easy to me.

Young and inexperienced, I thought the task easy.

* Without a friend to counsel him, the temptation proved irresistible.

Without a friend to counsel him, he found the temptation irresistible.

Sentences violating this rule are often ludicrous.

Being in a dilapidated condition, I was able to buy the house very cheap.

Divide words at line-ends, in accordance with their formation and pronunciation

If there is room at the end of a line for one or more syllables of a word, but not for the whole word, divide the word, unless this involves cutting off only a single letter, or cutting off only two letters of a long word. No hard and fast rule for all words can be laid down. The principles most frequently applicable are:

A. Divide the word according to its formation:

know-ledge (not knowl-edge)

Shake-speare (not Shakes-peare)

de-scribe (not des-cribe)

atmo-sphere (not atmos-phere)

B. Divide "on the vowel:"

edi-ble (not ed-ible)

ordi-nary

reli-gious

regu-lar

deco-rative

propo-sition

espe-cial

oppo-nents

classi-fi-ca-tion (three divisions possible)

presi-dent

C. Divide between double letters, unless they come at the end of the simple form of the word:

Apen-nines	Cincin-nati
refer-ring	tell-ing

The treatment of consonants in combination is best shown from examples:

for-tune	pic-ture
presump-tuous	illus-tration
sub-stan-tial (either division)	indus-try
instruc-tion	sug-ges-tion
incen-diary	

The student will do well to examine the syllable-division in a number of pages of any carefully printed book.

III

Elementary Principles of Composition

9. Make the paragraph the unit of composition: one paragraph to each topic

If the subject on which you are writing is of slight extent, or if you intend to treat it very briefly, there may be no need of subdividing it into topics. Thus a brief description, a brief summary of a literary work, a brief account of a single incident, a narrative merely outlining an action, the setting forth of a single idea, any one of these is best written in a single paragraph. After the paragraph has been written, it should be examined to see whether subdivision will not improve it.

Ordinarily, however, a subject requires subdivision into topics, each of which should be made the subject of a paragraph. The object of treating each topic in a paragraph by itself is, of course, to aid the reader. The beginning of each paragraph is a signal to him that a new step in the development of the subject has been reached.

The extent of subdivision will vary with the length of the composition. For example, a short notice of a book or poem might consist of a single paragraph. One slightly longer might consist of two paragraphs:

A. Account of the work.

B. Critical discussion.

A report on a poem, written for a class in literature, might consist of seven paragraphs:

A. Facts of composition and publication.

B. Kind of poem; metrical form.

C. Subject.

D. Treatment of subject.

E. For what chiefly remarkable.

F. Wherein characteristic of the writer.

G. Relationship to other works.

The contents of paragraphs C and D would vary with the poem. Usually, paragraph C would indicate the actual or imagined circumstances of the poem (the situation), if these call for explanation, and would then state the subject and outline its development. If the poem is a narrative in the third person throughout, paragraph C need contain no more than a concise summary of the action. Paragraph D would indicate the leading ideas and show how they are made prominent, or would indicate what points in the narrative are chiefly emphasized.

A novel might be discussed under the heads:

A. Setting.

B. Plot.

C. Characters.

D. Purpose.

A historical event might be discussed under the heads:

A. What led up to the event.

B. Account of the event.

C. What the event led up to.

In treating either of these last two subjects, the writer would probably find it necessary to subdivide one or more of the topics here given.

As a rule, single sentences should not be written or printed as paragraphs. An exception may be made of sentences of transition, indicating the relation between the parts of an exposition or argument.

In dialogue, each speech, even if only a single word, is a paragraph by itself; that is, a new paragraph begins with each change of speaker. The application of this rule, when dialogue and narrative are combined, is best learned from examples in well-printed works of fiction.

10. As a rule, begin each paragraph with a topic sentence; end it in conformity with the beginning

Again, the object is to aid the reader. The practice here recommended enables him to discover the purpose of each paragraph as he begins to read it, and to retain the purpose in mind as he ends it. For this reason, the most generally useful kind of paragraph, particularly in exposition and argument, is that in which

A. the topic sentence comes at or near the beginning;
B. the succeeding sentences explain or establish or develop the statement made in the topic sentence; and
C. the final sentence either emphasizes the thought of the topic sentence or states some important consequence.

Ending with a digression, or with an unimportant detail, is particularly to be avoided.

If the paragraph forms part of a larger composition, its relation to what precedes, or its function as a part of the whole, may need to be expressed. This can sometimes be done by a mere word or phrase (*again*; *therefore*; *for the same reason*) in the topic sentence. Sometimes, however, it is expedient to precede the topic sentence by one or more sentences of introduction or transition. If more than one such sentence is required, it is generally better to set apart the transitional sentences as a separate paragraph.

According to the writer's purpose, he may, as indicated above, relate the body of the paragraph to the topic sentence in one or more of several different ways. He may make the meaning of the topic sentence clearer by restating it in other forms, by defining its terms, by denying the converse, by giving illustrations or specific instances; he may establish it by proofs; or he may develop it by showing its implications and consequences. In a long paragraph, he may carry out several of these processes.

1. Now, to be properly enjoyed, a walking tour should be gone upon alone.

   Topic sentence.

2. If you go in a company, or even in pairs, it is no longer a walking tour in anything but name; it is something else and more in the nature of a picnic.

   The meaning made clearer by denial of the contrary.

3. A walking tour should be gone upon alone, because freedom is of the essence; because you should be able to stop and go on, and follow this way or that, as the freak takes you; and because you must have your own pace, and neither trot alongside a champion walker, nor mince in time with a girl.

The topic sentence repeated, in abridged form, and supported by three reasons; the meaning of the third ("you must have your own pace") made clearer by denying the converse.

4. And you must be open to all impressions and let your thoughts take colour from what you see.

   A fourth reason, stated in two forms.

5. You should be as a pipe for any wind to play upon.

   The same reason, stated in still another form.

6. "I cannot see the wit," says Hazlitt, "of walking and talking at the same time."

   The same reason as stated by Hazlitt.

7. When I am in the country, I wish to vegetate like the country, which is the gist of all that can be said upon the matter.

   The same reason as stated by Hazlitt.

8. There should be no cackle of voices at your elbow, to jar on the meditative silence of the morning.

   Repetition, in paraphrase, of the quotation from Hazlitt.

9. And so long as a man is reasoning he cannot surrender himself to that fine intoxication that comes of much motion in the open air, that begins in a sort of dazzle and sluggishness of the brain, and ends in a peace that passes comprehension. – Stevenson, *Walking Tours.*

   Final statement of the fourth reason, in language amplified and heightened to form a strong conclusion.

1. It was chiefly in the eighteenth century that a very different conception of history grew up.

   Topic sentence.

2. Historians then came to believe that their task was not so much to paint a picture as to solve a problem; to explain or illustrate the successive phases of national growth, prosperity, and adversity.

   The meaning of the topic sentence made clearer; the new conception of history defined.

3. The history of morals, of industry, of intellect, and of art; the changes that take place in manners or beliefs; the dominant ideas that prevailed in successive periods; the rise, fall, and modification of political constitutions; in a word, all the conditions of national well-being became the subject of their works.

   The definition expanded.

4. They sought rather to write a history of peoples than a history of kings.

   The definition explained by contrast.

5. They looked especially in history for the chain of causes and effects.

   The definition supplemented: another element in the new conception of history.

6. They undertook to study in the past the physiology of nations, and hoped by applying the experimental method on a large scale to deduce some lessons of real value about the condi-

tions on which the welfare of society mainly depend. – Lecky, *The Political Value of History*.

Conclusion: an important consequence of the new conception of history.

In narration and description the paragraph sometimes begins with a concise, comprehensive statement serving to hold together the details that follow.

The breeze served us admirably.

The campaign opened with a series of reverses.

The next ten or twelve pages were filled with a curious set of entries.

But this device, if too often used, would become a mannerism. More commonly the opening sentence simply indicates by its subject with what the paragraph is to be principally concerned.

At length I thought I might return towards the stockade.

He picked up the heavy lamp from the table and began to explore.

Another flight of steps, and they emerged on the roof.

The brief paragraphs of animated narrative, however, are often without even this semblance of a topic sentence. The break between them serves the purpose of a rhetorical pause, throwing into prominence some detail of the action.

11. Use the active voice

The active voice is usually more direct and vigorous than the passive:

> I shall always remember my first visit to Boston.

This is much better than

> My first visit to Boston will always be remembered by me.

The latter sentence is less direct, less bold, and less concise. If the writer tries to make it more concise by omitting "by me,"

> My first visit to Boston will always be remembered,

it becomes indefinite: is it the writer, or some person undisclosed, or the world at large, that will always remember this visit?

This rule does not, of course, mean that the writer should entirely discard the passive voice, which is frequently convenient and sometimes necessary.

> The dramatists of the Restoration are little esteemed today.
>
> Modern readers have little esteem for the dramatists of the Restoration.

The first would be the right form in a paragraph on the dramatists of the Restoration; the second, in a paragraph on the tastes of modern readers. The need of making a particular word the subject of the sentence will often, as in these examples, determine which voice is to be used.

The habitual use of the active voice, however, makes for forcible writing. This is true not only in narrative principally concerned with action, but in writing of any kind. Many a tame sentence of description or exposition can be made lively and emphatic by substituting a transitive in the active voice for some such perfunctory expression as *there is*, or *could be heard*.

> * There were a great number of dead leaves lying on the ground.
>
> Dead leaves covered the ground.
>
> * The sound of the falls could still be heard.
>
> The sound of the falls still reached our ears.
>
> * The reason that he left college was that his health became impaired.
>
> Failing health compelled him to leave college.
>
> * It was not long before he was very sorry that he had said what he had.
>
> He soon repented his words.

As a rule, avoid making one passive depend directly upon another.

* Gold was not allowed to be exported.

It was forbidden to export gold (The export of gold was prohibited).

* He has been proved to have been seen entering the building.

It has been proved that he was seen to enter the building.

In both the examples above, before correction, the word properly related to the second passive is made the subject of the first.

A common fault is to use as the subject of a passive construction a noun which expresses the entire action, leaving to the verb no function beyond that of completing the sentence.

* A survey of this region was made in 1900.

This region was surveyed in 1900.

* Mobilization of the army was rapidly carried out.

The army was rapidly mobilized.

* Confirmation of these reports cannot be obtained.

These reports cannot be confirmed.

Compare the sentence, "The export of gold was prohibited," in which the predicate "was prohibited" expresses something not implied in "export."

12. Put statements in positive form

Make definite assertions. Avoid tame, colorless, hesitating, non-committal language. Use the word *not* as a means of denial or in antithesis, never as a means of evasion.

> * He was not very often on time.
>
> He usually came late.

> * He did not think that studying Latin was much use.
>
> He thought the study of Latin useless.

> * *The Taming of the Shrew* is rather weak in spots. Shakespeare does not portray Katharine as a very admirable character, nor does Bianca remain long in memory as an important character in Shakespeare's works.
>
> The women in *The Taming of the Shrew* are unattractive. Katharine is disagreeable, Bianca insignificant.

The last example, before correction, is indefinite as well as negative. The corrected version, consequently, is simply a guess at the writer's intention.

All three examples show the weakness inherent in the word *not*. Consciously or unconsciously, the reader is dissatisfied with being told only what is not; he wishes to be told what is. Hence, as a rule, it is better to express a negative in positive form.

not honest	dishonest
not important	trifling
did not remember	forgot
did not pay any attention to	ignored
did not have much confidence in	distrusted

The antithesis of negative and positive is strong:

Not charity, but simple justice.

Not that I loved Caesar less, but Rome the more.

Negative words other than *not* are usually strong:

The sun never sets upon the British flag.

13. Omit needless words

Vigorous writing is concise. A sentence should contain no unnecessary words, a paragraph no unnecessary sentences, for the same reason that a drawing should have no unnecessary lines and a machine no unnecessary parts. This requires not that the writer make all his sentences short, or that he avoid all detail and treat his subjects only in outline, but that every word tell.

Many expressions in common use violate this principle:

* the question as to whether	whether (the question whether)
* there is no doubt but that	no doubt (doubtless)
* used for fuel purposes	used for fuel
* he is a man who	he
* in a hasty manner	hastily
* this is a subject which	this subject
* His story is a strange one.	His story is strange.

In especial the expression *the fact that* should be revised out of every sentence in which it occurs.

* owing to the fact that
  since (because)

* in spite of the fact that
  though (although)

* call your attention to the fact that
  remind you (notify you)

* I was unaware of the fact that
  I was unaware that (did not know)

* the fact that he had not succeeded
  his failure

* the fact that I had arrived
  my arrival

See also under *case*, *character*, *nature*, *system* in Chapter V.

Who is, *which was*, and the like are often superfluous.

* His brother, who is a member of the same firm
  His brother, a member of the same firm

* Trafalgar, which was Nelson's last battle
  Trafalgar, Nelson's last battle

As positive statement is more concise than negative, and the active voice more concise than the passive, many of the examples given under Rules 11 and 12 illustrate this rule as well.

A common violation of conciseness is the presentation of a single complex idea, step by step, in a series of sentences which might to advantage be combined into one.

> * Macbeth was very ambitious. This led him to wish to become king of Scotland. The witches told him that this wish of his would come true. The king of Scotland at this time was Duncan. Encouraged by his wife, Macbeth murdered Duncan. He was thus enabled to succeed Duncan as king. (55 words.)

> Encouraged by his wife, Macbeth achieved his ambition and realized the prediction of the witches by murdering Duncan and becoming king of Scotland in his place. (26 words.)

14. Avoid a succession of loose sentences

This rule refers especially to loose sentences of a particular type, those consisting of two co-ordinate clauses, the second introduced by a conjunction or relative. Although single sentences of this type may be unexceptionable (see under Rule 4), a series soon becomes monotonous and tedious.

An unskilful writer will sometimes construct a whole paragraph of sentences of this kind, using as connectives *and*, *but*, and less frequently, *who*, *which*, *when*, *where*, and *while*, these last in non-restrictive senses (see under Rule 3).

> The third concert of the subscription series was given last evening, and a large audience was in attendance. Mr. Edward Appleton was the soloist, and the Boston Symphony Orchestra furnished the instrumental music. The former showed himself to be an artist of the first rank, while the latter proved itself fully deserving of its high reputation. The interest aroused by the series has been very gratifying to the Committee, and it is planned to give a similar series annually hereafter. The fourth concert will be given on Tuesday, May 10, when an equally attractive programme will be presented.

Apart from its triteness and emptiness, the paragraph above is bad because of the structure of its sentences, with their mechanical symmetry and sing-song. Contrast with them the sentences in the paragraphs quoted under Rule 10, or in any piece of good English prose, as the preface (Before the Curtain) to *Vanity Fair*.

If the writer finds that he has written a series of sentences of the type described, he should recast enough of them to remove the monotony, replacing them by simple sentences, by sentences of two clauses joined by a semicolon, by periodic sentences of two clauses, by sentences, loose or periodic, of three clauses - whichever best represent the real relations of the thought.

15. Express co-ordinate ideas in similar form

This principle, that of parallel construction, requires that expressions of similar content and function should be outwardly similar. The likeness of form enables the reader to recognize more readily the likeness of content and function. Familiar instances from the Bible are the Ten Commandments, the Beatitudes, and the petitions of the Lord's Prayer.

The unskilful writer often violates this principle, from a mistaken belief that he should constantly vary the form of his expressions. It is true that in repeating a statement in order to emphasize it he may have need to vary its form. For illustration, see the paragraph from Stevenson quoted under Rule 10. But apart from this, he should follow the principle of parallel construction.

* Formerly, science was taught by the textbook method, while now the laboratory method is employed.	Formerly, science was taught by the textbook method; now it is taught by the laboratory method.

The left-hand version gives the impression that the writer is undecided or timid; he seems unable or afraid to choose one form of expression and hold to it. The right-hand version shows that the writer has at least made his choice and abided by it.

By this principle, an article or a preposition applying to all the members of a series must either be used only before the first term or else be repeated before each term.

> * The French, the Italians, Spanish, and Portuguese
>
> The French, the Italians, the Spanish, and the Portuguese

> * In spring, summer, or in winter
>
> In spring, summer, or winter (In spring, in summer, or in winter)

Correlative expressions (*both*, *and*; *not*, *but*; *not only*, *but also*; *either*, *or*; *first*, *second*, *third*; and the like) should be followed by the same grammatical construction. Many violations of this rule can be corrected by rearranging the sentence.

> * It was both a long ceremony and very tedious.
>
> The ceremony was both long and tedious.

> * A time not for words, but action.
>
> A time not for words, but for action.

> * Either you must grant his request or incur his ill will.
>
> You must either grant his request or incur his ill will.

* My objections are, first, the injustice of the measure; second, that it is unconstitutional.

My objections are, first, that the measure is unjust; second, that it is unconstitutional.

See also the third example under Rule 12 and the last under Rule 13.

It may be asked, what if a writer needs to express a very large number of similar ideas, say twenty? Must he write twenty consecutive sentences of the same pattern? On closer examination he will probably find that the difficulty is imaginary, that his twenty ideas can be classified in groups, and that he need apply the principle only within each group. Otherwise he had best avoid the difficulty by putting his statements in the form of a table.

16. Keep related words together

The position of the words in a sentence is the principal means of showing their relationship. The writer must therefore, so far as possible, bring together the words, and groups of words, that are related in thought, and keep apart those which are not so related.

The subject of a sentence and the principal verb should not, as a rule, be separated by a phrase or clause that can be transferred to the beginning.

* Wordsworth, in the fifth book of *The Excursion*, gives a minute description of this church.

In the fifth book of *The Excursion*, Wordsworth gives a minute description of this church.

* Cast iron, when treated in a Bessemer converter, is changed into steel.

By treatment in a Bessemer converter, cast iron is changed into steel.

The objection is that the interposed phrase or clause needlessly interrupts the natural order of the main clause. This objection, however, does not usually hold when the order is interrupted only by a relative clause or by an expression in apposition. Nor does it hold in periodic sentences in which the interruption is a deliberately used means of creating suspense (see examples under Rule 18).

The relative pronoun should come, as a rule, immediately after its antecedent.

* There was a look in his eye that boded mischief.

In his eye was a look that boded mischief.

* He wrote three articles about his adventures in Spain, which were published in *Harper's Magazine.*

He published in *Harper's Magazine* three articles about his adventures in Spain.

* This is a portrait of Benjamin Harrison, grandson of William Henry Harrison, who became President in 1889.

This is a portrait of Benjamin Harrison, grandson of William Henry Harrison. He became President in 1889.

If the antecedent consists of a group of words, the relative comes at the end of the group, unless this would cause ambiguity.

The Superintendent of the Chicago Division, who

* A proposal to amend the Sherman Act, which has been variously judged

A proposal, which has been variously judged, to amend the Sherman Act

A proposal to amend the much-debated Sherman Act

* The grandson of William Henry Harrison, who

William Henry Harrison's grandson, Benjamin Harrison, who

A noun in apposition may come between antecedent and relative, because in such a combination no real ambiguity can arise.

The Duke of York, his brother, who was regarded with hostility by the Whigs

Modifiers should come, if possible next to the word they modify. If several expressions modify the same word, they should be so arranged that no wrong relation is suggested.

* All the members were not present.

Not all the members were present.

* He only found two mistakes.

He found only two mistakes.

* Major R. E. Joyce will give a lecture on Tuesday evening in Bailey Hall, to which the public is invited, on "My Experiences in Mesopotamia" at eight P. M.

On Tuesday evening at eight P. M., Major R. E. Joyce will give in Bailey Hall a lecture on "My Experiences in Mesopotamia". The public is invited.

17. In summaries, keep to one tense

In summarizing the action of a drama, the writer should always use the present tense. In summarizing a poem, story, or novel, he should preferably use the present, though he may use the past if he prefers. If the summary is in the present tense, antecedent action should be expressed by the perfect; if in the past, by the past perfect.

> An unforeseen chance prevents Friar John from delivering Friar Lawrence's letter to Romeo. Juliet, meanwhile, owing to her father's arbitrary change of the day set for her wedding, has been compelled to drink the potion on Tuesday night, with the result that Balthasar informs Romeo of her supposed death before Friar Lawrence learns of the nondelivery of the letter.

But whichever tense be used in the summary, a past tense in indirect discourse or in indirect question remains unchanged.

> The Legate inquires who struck the blow.

Apart from the exceptions noted, whichever tense the writer chooses, he should use throughout. Shifting from one tense to the other gives the appearance of uncertainty and irresolution (compare Rule 15).

In presenting the statements or the thought of some one else, as in summarizing an essay or reporting a speech, the writer should avoid intercalating such expressions as "he said," "he stated," "the speaker added," "the speaker then went on to say," "the author also thinks," or the like. He should indicate clearly at the outset, once for all, that what follows is summary, and then waste no words in repeating the notification.

In notebooks, in newspapers, in handbooks of literature, summaries of one kind or another may be indispensable, and for children in primary schools it is a useful exercise to retell a story in their own words. But in the criticism or interpretation of literature the writer should be careful to avoid dropping into summary. He may find it necessary to devote one or two sentences to indicating the subject, or the opening situation, of the work he is discussing; he may cite numerous details to illustrate its qualities. But he should aim to write an orderly discussion supported by evidence, not a summary with occasional comment. Similarly, if the scope of his discussion includes a number of works, he will as a rule do better not to take them up singly in chronological order, but to aim from the beginning at establishing general conclusions.

18. Place the emphatic words of a sentence at the end

The proper place for the word, or group of words, which the writer desires to make most prominent is usually the end of the sentence.

> * Humanity has hardly advanced in fortitude since that time, though it has advanced in many other ways.
>
> Humanity, since that time, has advanced in many other ways, but it has hardly advanced in fortitude.

> * This steel is principally used for making razors, because of its hardness.
>
> Because of its hardness, this steel is principally used in making razors.

The word or group of words entitled to this position of prominence is usually the logical predicate, that is, the new element in the sentence, as it is in the second example.

The effectiveness of the periodic sentence arises from the prominence which it gives to the main statement.

> Four centuries ago, Christopher Columbus, one of the Italian mariners whom the decline of their own republics had put at the service of the world and of adventure, seeking for Spain a westward passage to the Indies as a set-off against the achievements of Portuguese discoverers, lighted on America.

> With these hopes and in this belief I would urge you, laying aside all hindrance, thrusting away all private aims, to devote yourself unswervingly and unflinchingly to the vigorous and successful prosecution of this war.

The other prominent position in the sentence is the beginning. Any element in the sentence, other than the subject, becomes emphatic when placed first.

> Deceit or treachery he could never forgive.

> So vast and rude, fretted by the action of nearly three thousand years, the fragments of this architecture may often seem, at first sight, like works of nature.

A subject coming first in its sentence may be emphatic, but hardly by its position alone. In the sentence,

> Great kings worshipped at his shrine,

the emphasis upon kings arises largely from its meaning and from the context. To receive special emphasis, the subject of a sentence must take the position of the predicate.

> Through the middle of the valley flowed a winding stream.

The principle that the proper place for what is to be made most prominent is the end applies equally to the words of a sentence, to the sentences of a paragraph, and to the paragraphs of a composition.

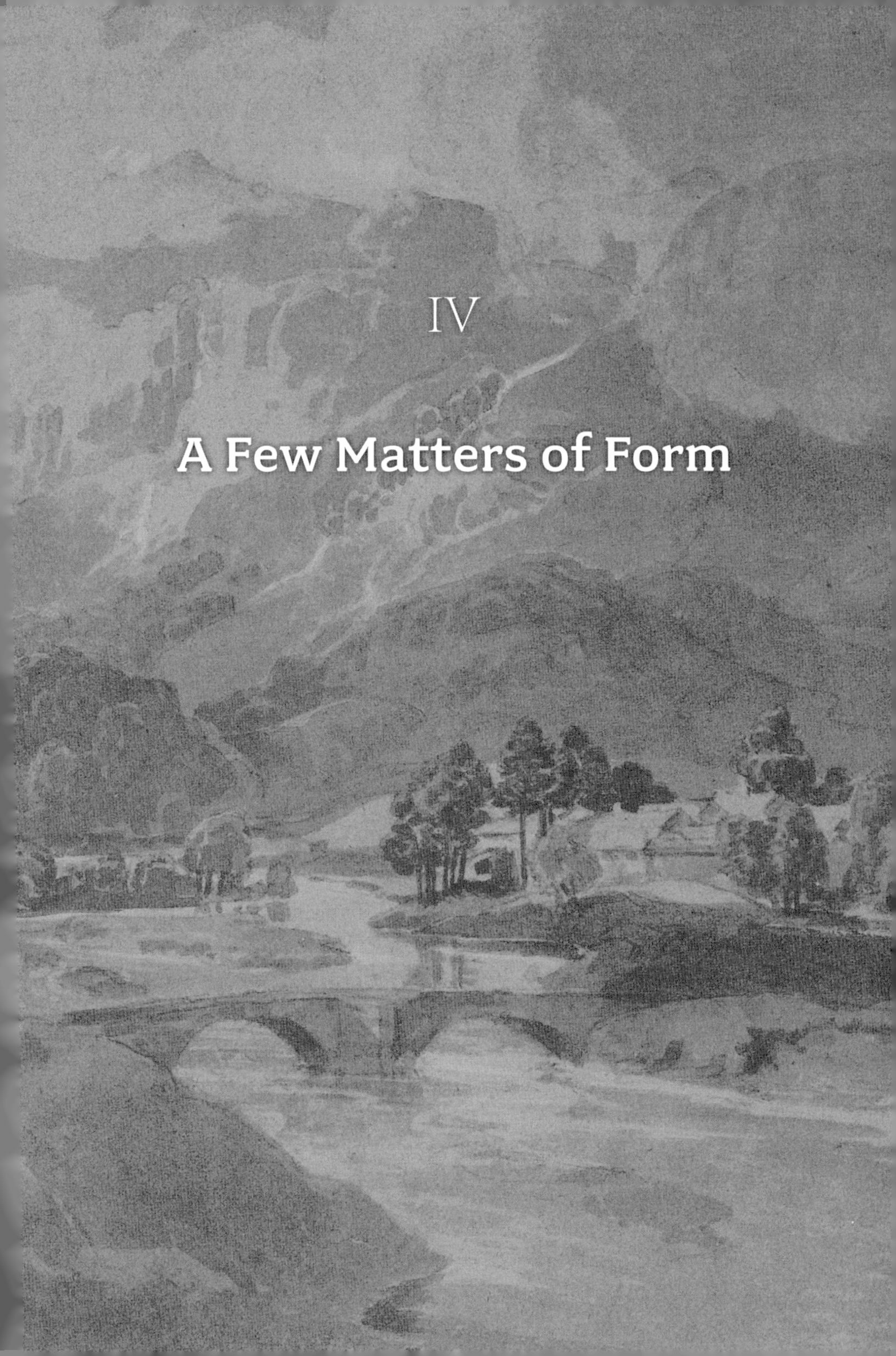

IV

A Few Matters of Form

1. Headings.

Leave a blank line, or its equivalent in space, after the title or heading of a manuscript. On succeeding pages, if using ruled paper, begin on the first line.

2. Numerals.

Do not spell out dates or other serial numbers. Write them in figures or in Roman notation, as may be appropriate.

August 9, 1918	Chapter XII
Rule 3	352d Infantry

3. Parentheses.

A sentence containing an expression in parenthesis is punctuated, outside of the marks of parenthesis, exactly as if the expression in parenthesis were absent. The expression within is punctuated as if it stood by itself, except that the final stop is omitted unless it is a question mark or an exclamation point.

> I went to his house yesterday (my third attempt to see him), but he had left town.

> He declares (and why should we doubt his good faith?) that he is now certain of success.

(When a wholly detached expression or sentence is parenthesized, the final stop comes before the last mark of parenthesis.)

4. Quotations.

Formal quotations, cited as documentary evidence, are introduced by a colon and enclosed in quotation marks.

> The provision of the Constitution is: "No tax or duty shall be laid on articles exported from any state."

Quotations grammatically in apposition or the direct objects of verbs are preceded by a comma and enclosed in quotation marks.

> I recall the maxim of La Rochefoucauld, "Gratitude is a lively sense of benefits to come."
>
> Aristotle says, "Art is an imitation of nature."

Quotations of an entire line, or more, of verse, are begun on a fresh line and centered, but not enclosed in quotation marks.

> Wordsworth's enthusiasm for the Revolution was at first unbounded:
>
> Bliss was it in that dawn to be alive,
> But to be young was very heaven!

Quotations introduced by *that* are regarded as in indirect discourse and not enclosed in quotation marks.

> Keats declares that beauty is truth, truth beauty.

Proverbial expressions and familiar phrases of literary origin require no quotation marks.

These are the times that try men's souls.

He lives far from the madding crowd.

The same is true of colloquialisms and slang.

5. References.

In scholarly work requiring exact references, abbreviate titles that occur frequently, giving the full forms in an alphabetical list at the end. As a general practice, give the references in parenthesis or in footnotes, not in the body of the sentence. Omit the words *act*, *scene*, *line*, *book*, *volume*, *page*, except when referring by only one of them. Punctuate as indicated below.

* In the second scene of the third act

In III.ii (still better, simply insert III.ii in parenthesis at the proper place in the sentence)

After the killing of Polonius, Hamlet is placed under guard (IV. ii.14).

2 *Samuel* i.17–27

Othello II.iii.264–267, III.iii.155–161

6. Titles.

For the titles of literary works, scholarly usage prefers italics with capitalized initials. The usage of editors and publishers varies, some using italics with capitalized initials, others using Roman with capitalized initials and with or without quotation marks. Use italics (indicated in manuscript by underscoring), except in writing for a periodical that follows a different practice. Omit initial *A* or *The* from titles when you place the possessive before them.

> *The Iliad; the Odyssey; As You Like It; To a Skylark; The Newcomes; A Tale of Two Cities; Dickens's Tale of Two Cities.*

V

Words and Expressions Commonly Misused

(Many of the words and expressions here listed are not so much bad English as bad style, the commonplaces of careless writing. As illustrated under *Feature*, the proper correction is likely to be not the replacement of one word or set of words by another, but the replacement of vague generality by definite statement.)

1. All right.

Idiomatic in familiar speech as a detached phrase in the sense, "Agreed," or "Go ahead." In other uses better avoided. Always written as two words.

2. As good or better than.

Expressions of this type should be corrected by rearranging the sentence.

> * My opinion is as good or better than his.
>
> My opinion is as good as his, or better (if not better).

3. As to whether.

Whether is sufficient; see under Rule 13.

4. Bid.

Takes the infinitive without *to*. The past tense is *bade*.

5. Case.

The *Concise Oxford Dictionary* begins its definition of this word: "instance of a thing's occurring; usual state of affairs." In these two senses, the word is usually unnecessary.

> * In many cases, the rooms were poorly ventilated.
>
> Many of the rooms were poorly ventilated.

> * It has rarely been the case that any mistake has been made.
>
> Few mistakes have been made.

See Wood, *Suggestions to Authors*, pp. 68-71, and Quiller-Couch, *The Art of Writing*, pp. 103-106.

6. Certainly.

Used indiscriminately by some speakers, much as others use *very*, to intensify any and every statement. A mannerism of this kind, bad in speech, is even worse in writing.

7. Character.

Often simply redundant, used from a mere habit of wordiness.

> * acts of a hostile character
>
> hostile acts

8. Claim, vb.

With object-noun, means *lay claim to*. May be used with a dependent clause if this sense is clearly involved: "He claimed that he was the sole surviving heir." (But even here, "claimed to be" would be better.) Not to be used as a substitute for *declare*, *maintain*, or *charge*.

9. Compare.

To *compare to* is to point out or imply resemblances, between objects regarded as essentially of different order; to *compare with* is mainly to point out differences, between objects regarded as essentially of the same order. Thus life has been compared to a pilgrimage, to a drama, to a battle; Congress may be compared with the British Parliament. Paris has been compared to ancient Athens; it may be compared with modern London.

10. Clever.

This word has been greatly overused; it is best restricted to ingenuity displayed in small matters.

11. Consider.

Not followed by *as* when it means, "believe to be." "I consider him thoroughly competent." Compare, "The lecturer considered Cromwell first as soldier and second as administrator," where "considered" means "examined" or "discussed."

12. Dependable.

A needless substitute for *reliable*, *trustworthy*.

13. Due to.

Incorrectly used for *through*, *because of*, or *owing to*, in adverbial phrases: "He lost the first game, due to carelessness." In correct use related as predicate or as modifier to a particular noun: "This invention is due to Edison;" "losses due to preventable fires."

14. Effect.

As noun, means *result*; as verb, means *to bring about*, *accomplish* (not to be confused with *affect*, which means "to influence").

As noun, often loosely used in perfunctory writing about fashions, music, painting, and other arts: "an Oriental effect;" "effects in pale green;" "very delicate effects;" "broad effects;" "subtle effects;" "a charming effect was produced by." The writer who has a definite meaning to express will not take refuge in such vagueness.

15. Etc.

Not to be used of persons. Equivalent to *and the rest*, *and so forth*, and hence not to be used if one of these would be insufficient, that is, if the reader would be left in doubt as to any important particulars. Least open to objection when it represents the last terms of a list already given in full, or immaterial words at the end of a quotation.

At the end of a list introduced by *such as*, *for example*, or any similar expression, *etc.* is incorrect.

16. Fact.

Use this word only of matters of a kind capable of direct verification, not of matters of judgment. That a particular event happened on a given date, that lead melts at a certain temperature, are facts. But such conclusions as that Napoleon was the greatest of modern generals, or that the climate of California is delightful, however incontestable they may be, are not properly facts.

On the formula *the fact that*, see under Rule 13.

17. Factor.

A hackneyed word; the expressions of which it forms part can usually be replaced by something more direct and idiomatic.

> * His superior training was the great factor in his winning the match.
>
> He won the match by being better trained.

> * Heavy artillery is becoming an increasingly important factor in deciding battles.
>
> Heavy artillery is playing a larger and larger part in deciding battles.

18. Feature.

Another hackneyed word; like *factor* it usually adds nothing to the sentence in which it occurs.

> *A feature of the entertainment especially worthy of mention was the singing of Miss A.
>
> (Better use the same number of words to tell what Miss A. sang, or if the programme has already been given, to tell something of how she sang.)

As a verb, in the advertising sense of *offer as a special attraction*, to be avoided.

19. Fix.

Colloquial in America for *arrange*, *prepare*, *mend*. In writing restrict it to its literary senses, *fasten*, *make firm* or *immovable*, etc.

20. He is a man who.

A common type of redundant expression; see Rule 13.

> *He is a man who is very ambitious.
>
> He is very ambitious.

> *Spain is a country which I have always wanted to visit.
>
> I have always wanted to visit Spain.

21. However.

In the meaning *nevertheless*, not to come first in its sentence or clause.

> * The roads were almost impassable. However, we at last succeeded in reaching camp.
>
> The roads were almost impassable. At last, however, we succeeded in reaching camp.

When *however* comes first, it means *in whatever way* or *to whatever extent.*

> However you advise him, he will probably do as he thinks best.
>
> However discouraging the prospect, he never lost heart.

22. Kind of.

Not to be used as a substitute for *rather* (before adjectives and verbs), or except in familiar style, for *something like* (before nouns). Restrict it to its literal sense: "Amber is a kind of fossil resin;" "I dislike that kind of notoriety." The same holds true of *sort of*.

23. Less.

Should not be misused for *fewer*.

* He had less men than in the previous campaign.

He had fewer men than in the previous campaign.

Less refers to quantity, *fewer* to number. "His troubles are less than mine" means "His troubles are not so great as mine." "His troubles are fewer than mine" means "His troubles are not so numerous as mine." It is, however, correct to say, "The signers of the petition were less than a hundred," where the round number, a hundred, is something like a collective noun, and *less* is thought of as meaning a less quantity or amount.

24. Line, along these lines.

Line in the sense of *course of procedure*, *conduct*, *thought*, is allowable, but has been so much overworked, particularly in the phrase *along these lines*, that a writer who aims at freshness or originality had better discard it entirely.

* Mr. B. also spoke along the same lines.

Mr. B. also spoke, to the same effect.

* He is studying along the line of French literature.

He is studying French literature.

25. Literal, literally.

Often incorrectly used in support of exaggeration or violent metaphor.

> * a literal flood of abuse
> a flood of abuse

> * literally dead with fatigue
> almost dead with fatigue (dead tired)

26. Lose out.

Meant to be more emphatic than *lose*, but actually less so, because of its commonness. The same holds true of *try out*, *win out*, *sign up*, *register up*. With a number of verbs, *out* and *up* form idiomatic combinations: *find out*, *run out*, *turn out*, *cheer up*, *dry up*, *make up*, and others, each distinguishable in meaning from the simple verb. *Lose out* is not.

27. Most.

Not to be used for *almost*.

> * most everybody
> almost everybody

> * most all the time
> almost all the time

28. Nature.

Often simply redundant, used like *character*.

> * acts of a hostile nature
>
> hostile acts

Often vaguely used in such expressions as "a lover of nature;" "poems about nature." Unless more specific statements follow, the reader cannot tell whether the poems have to do with natural scenery, rural life, the sunset, the untracked wilderness, or the habits of squirrels.

29. Near by.

Adverbial phrase, not yet fully accepted as good English, though the analogy of *close by* and *hard by* seems to justify it. *Near*, or *near at hand*, is as good, if not better.

Not to be used as an adjective; use *neighboring*.

30. Oftentimes, ofttimes.

Archaic forms, no longer in good use. The modern word is *often*.

31. One hundred and one.

Retain the *and* in this and similar expressions, in accordance with the unvarying usage of English prose from Old English times.

32. One of the most.

Avoid beginning essays or paragraphs with this formula, as, "One of the most interesting developments of modern science is, etc.;" "Switzerland is one of the most interesting countries of Europe." There is nothing wrong in this; it is simply threadbare and forcible-feeble.

33. People.

The people is a political term, not to be confused with *the public*. From the people comes political support or opposition; from the public comes artistic appreciation or commercial patronage.

The word *people* is not to be used with words of number, in place of *persons*. If of "six people" five went away, how many "people" would be left?

34. Phase.

Means a stage of transition or development: "the phases of the moon;" "the last phase." Not to be used for *aspect* or *topic*.

* another phase of the subject
  another point (another question)

35. Possess.

Not to be used as a mere substitute for *have* or *own*.

* He possessed great courage.
  He had great courage (was very brave).

* He was the fortunate possessor of
  He owned

36. Respective, respectively.

These words may usually be omitted with advantage.

* Works of fiction are listed under the names of their respective authors.
  Works of fiction are listed under the names of their authors.

* The one mile and two mile runs were won by Jones and Cummings respectively.
  The one mile and two mile runs were won by Jones and by Cummings.

In some kinds of formal writing, as in geometrical proofs, it may be necessary to use *respectively*, but it should not appear in writing on ordinary subjects.

37. So.

Avoid, in writing, the use of *so* as an intensifier: "so good;" "so warm;" "so delightful."

On the use of *so* to introduce clauses, see Rule 4.

38. Sort of.

See under *kind of*.

39. State.

Not to be used as a mere substitute for *say*, *remark*. Restrict it to the sense of *express fully or clearly*, as, "He refused to state his objections."

40. Student Body.

A needless and awkward expression, meaning no more than the simple word *students*.

* a member of the student body
  a student

* popular with the student body
  liked by the students

* The student body passed resolutions.
  The students passed resolutions.

41. System.

Frequently used without need.

* Dayton has adopted the commission system of government.
  Dayton has adopted government by commission.

* the dormitory system
  dormitories

42. Thanking you in advance.

This sounds as if the writer meant, "It will not be worth my while to write to you again." Simply write, "Thanking you," and if the favor which you have requested is granted, write a letter of acknowledgement.

43. They.

A common inaccuracy is the use of the plural pronoun when the antecedent is a distributive expression such as *each*, *each one*, *everybody*, *every one*, *many a man*, which, though implying more than one person, requires the pronoun to be in the singular. Similar to this, but with even less justification, is the use of the plural pronoun with the antecedent *anybody*, *any one*, *somebody*, *some one*, the intention being either to avoid the awkward "he or she," or to avoid committing oneself to either. Some bashful speakers even say, "A friend of mine told me that they, etc."

Use *he* with all the above words, unless the antecedent is or must be feminine.

44. Very.

Use this word sparingly. Where emphasis is necessary, use words strong in themselves.

45. Viewpoint.

Write *point of view*, but do not misuse this, as many do, for *view* or *opinion*.

46. While.

Avoid the indiscriminate use of this word for *and*, *but*, and *although*. Many writers use it frequently as a substitute for *and* or *but*, either from a mere desire to vary the connective, or from uncertainty which of the two connectives is the more appropriate. In this use it is best replaced by a semicolon.

This is entirely correct, as shown by the paraphrase,

> * The office and salesrooms are on the ground floor, while the rest of the building is devoted to manufacturing.
>
> The office and salesrooms are on the ground floor; the rest of the building is devoted to manufacturing.

Its use as a virtual equivalent of *although* is allowable in sentences where this leads to no ambiguity or absurdity.

> While I admire his energy, I wish it were employed in a better cause.
>
> I admire his energy; at the same time I wish it were employed in a better cause.

Compare:

> * While the temperature reaches 90 or 95 degrees in the daytime, the nights are often chilly.
>
> Although the temperature reaches 90 or 95 degrees in the daytime, the nights are often chilly.

The paraphrase,

> The temperature reaches 90 or 95 degrees in the daytime; at the same time the nights are often chilly,

shows why the use of *while* is incorrect.

In general, the writer will do well to use *while* only with strict literalness, in the sense of *during the time that.*

47. Whom.

Often incorrectly used for *who* before *he said* or similar expressions, when it is really the subject of a following verb.

> * His brother, whom he said would send him the money
>
> His brother, who he said would send him the money

> * The man whom he thought was his friend
>
> The man who (that) he thought was his friend (whom he thought his friend)

48. Worth while.

Overworked as a term of vague approval and (with *not*) of disapproval. Strictly applicable only to actions: "Is it worth while to telegraph?"

> * His books are not worth while.
>
> His books are not worth reading (not worth one's while to read; do not repay reading).

The use of *worth while* before a noun ("a worth while story") is indefensible.

49. Would.

A conditional statement in the first person requires *should*, not *would*.

> I should not have succeeded without his help.

The equivalent of *shall* in indirect quotation after a verb in the past tense is *should*, not *would*.

> He predicted that before long we should have a great surprise.

To express habitual or repeated action, the past tense, without *would*, is usually sufficient, and from its brevity, more emphatic.

> * Once a year he would visit the old mansion.
>
> Once a year he visited the old mansion.

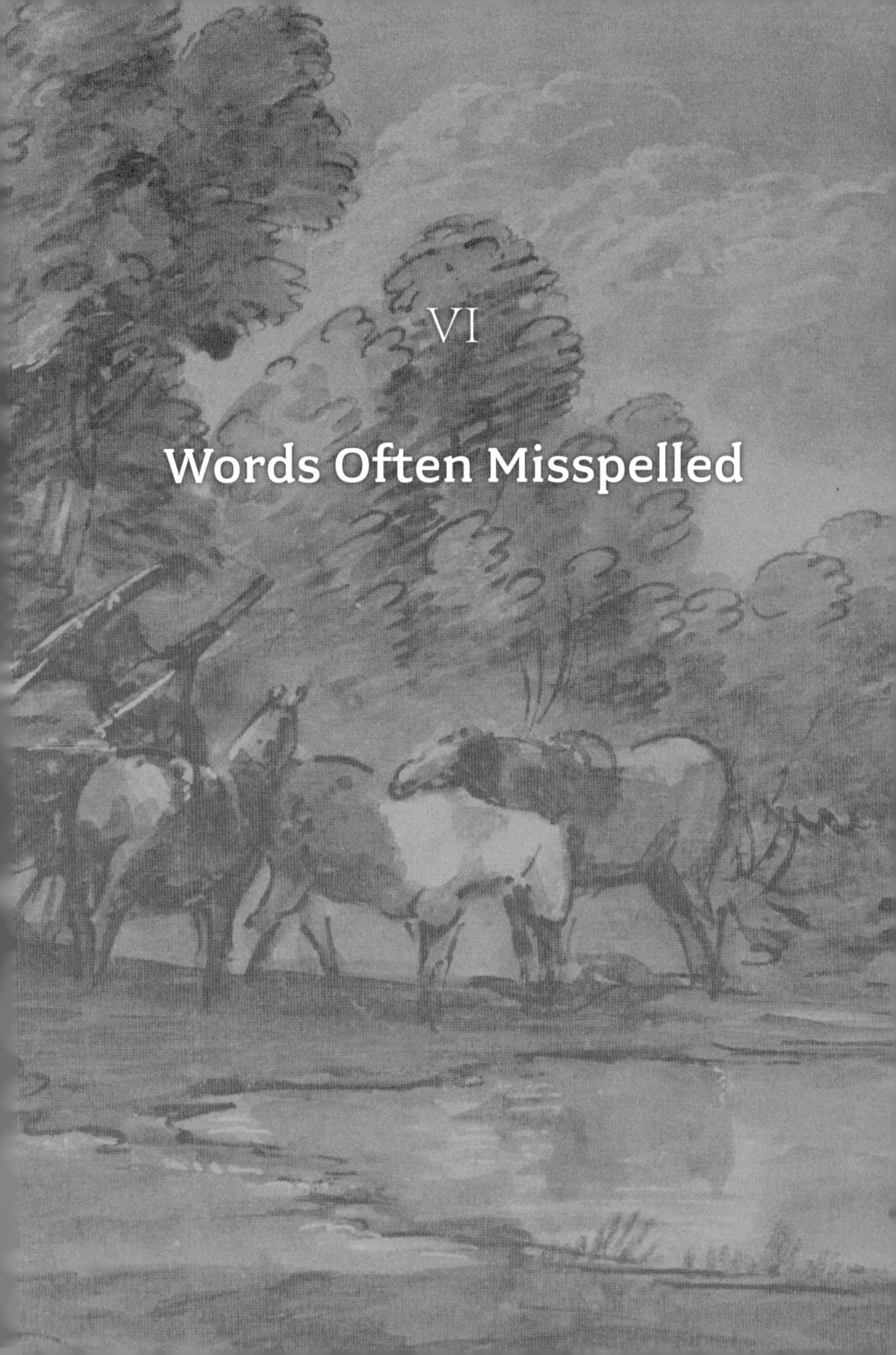

VI

Words Often Misspelled

accidentally
advice
affect
beginning
believe
benefit
challenge
criticize
deceive
definite
describe
despise
develop
disappoint
duel
ecstasy
effect
existence
fiery
formerly
humorous
hypocrisy
immediately
incidentally
latter
led
lose
marriage
mischief
murmur
necessary
occurred
parallel
Philip
playwright
preceding
prejudice
principal
privilege
pursue
repetition
rhyme
rhythm
ridiculous
sacrilegious
seize
separate
shepherd
siege
similar
simile
too
tragedy
tries
undoubtedly
until

目　錄

I. 引言 87

II. 英文用法八大規則 91

1. 在單數名詞後加「's」，構成名詞所有格 93
2. 連續使用三個或以上的字詞，在最後一個字詞前使用連詞，其餘的以逗號分隔 94
3. 插入語要放在兩個逗號之間 95
4. 以連詞 and 或 but 引出獨立分句，要在 and 或 but 前標示逗號 98
5. 不要用逗號直接連接獨立分句 100
6. 不要將一個完整的句子拆成兩句 102
7. 句首的分詞短語所指涉的主語要和主句主語保持一致 103
8. 行末斷字時要遵守字的組成和發音規則 105

III. 英文寫作十大原則 107

9. 以段落為基礎單位，一段一主題 109
10. 每段以主題句開始，段尾要與段首呼應 112
11. 使用主動語態 117
12. 用肯定句陳述 121
13. 刪去贅字 124
14. 避免使用一連串結構鬆散的句子 129
15. 使用相似的句型結構表達對等的概念 131

16. 相關的字詞要放在一起 134
17. 用同一種時態寫撮要 138
18. 強調的字眼要放在句末 140

IV. **格式注意事項** 143

V. **常見誤用字詞和短語** 151

VI. **經常拼錯的單字** 175

I

引言

本書原意是為文學賞析課程中的寫作練習提供輔導材料，旨在以簡明扼要的語言為讀者提供平實的英文寫作風格之要素，以減輕教師和學生的負擔。為此，本書圍繞幾個要點，舉例說明了語法和寫作上常見的錯誤（見第二章和第三章）。章節的規則編號可在校閱文稿時對照使用。

本書只涵蓋了英文寫作風格的一小部份。根據筆者的經驗，學生吸收了這些概要知識後，想要獲得更大的收益，就必須根據其自身的弱點得到個別的指引；教師也更傾向於使用自己的理論來教導寫作，而不是使用其他的教科書。

非常感謝康乃爾大學英文部的同事在筆者寫作原稿時給予了極大的幫助。感謝佐治・麥蘭・伍德先生慷慨同意本書將其著作《給作者的建議》的部份內容納入本書規則十一。

推薦以下書目供讀者參考或進行延伸閱讀：

第二章及第四章的相關參考書目：

F. Howard Collins, *Author and Printer* (Henry Frowde)

Chicago University Press, *Manual of Style*

T. L. De Vinne, *Correct Composition* (The Century Company)

Horace Hart, *Rules for Compositors and Printers* (Oxford University Press)

George McLane Wood, *Extracts from the Style-Book of the Government Printing Office* (United States Geological Survey)

第三章及第五章的相關參考書目：

Sir Arthur Quiller-Couch, *The Art of Writing* (Putnams)，特別是 Interlude on Jargon 這章

George McLane Wood, *Suggestions to Authors* (United States Geological Survey)

John Leslie Hall, *English Usage* (Scott, Foresman and Co.)

James P. Kelly, *Workmanship in Words* (Little, Brown and Co.)

根據以往的觀察，最頂尖的作家有時也會刻意忽略修辭規則，而這些「違規」的表達會令讀者感覺耳目一新。然而，除非作者確信自己能達到同樣的水平，否則寫作時最好還是依規則而行。當作者在規則的指引下，寫出了日常生活中要求的平實英文之後，他們就可以多多拜讀文學大師的作品，進而探尋不同寫作風格之奧妙。

II

英文用法八大規則

1. 在單數名詞後加「's」，構成名詞所有格

此規則適用於以各種子音結尾的單數名詞，例如：

Charles's friend	查爾斯的朋友
Burns's poems	伯恩斯的詩歌
the witch's malice	女巫的歹毒心腸

這是美國政府出版機構和牛津大學出版社的常規用法。

例外情況如下：以 -es 和 -is 結尾的古代專有名詞（其所有格只需加「'」），以及 Jesus' 和類似 for conscience' sake、for righteousness' sake 的詞組。但是像 Achilles' heel、Moses' laws、Isis' temple 這類型的所有格，通常由以下形式替代：

the heel of Achilles	阿基里斯的腳踝
the laws of Moses	摩西的法則
the temple of Isis	伊西神殿

所有格代詞 hers、its、theirs、yours 和 oneself 等無需使用撇號「'」。

連續使用三個或以上的字詞，在最後一個字詞前使用連詞，其餘的以逗號分隔

例如：

red, white, and blue
紅、白、藍

honest, energetic, but headstrong
誠實、精力充沛、但剛愎自用

He opened the letter, read it, and made a note of its contents.
他打開信，看完以後，又在信上做了筆記。

這也是美國政府出版機構和牛津大學出版社的常規用法。

在公司名稱中，連接詞前的最後一個逗號需要刪去，如：

Brown, Shipley and Company
布朗士普利公司

縮寫字 etc. 之前必須使用逗號，即使它的前面只列出了一個字詞。

3. 插入語要放在兩個逗號之間

The best way to see a country, unless you are pressed for time, is to travel on foot.

如果不趕時間，遊覽國家最好的方法就是步行。

此規則較難應用：人們總覺得難以判斷一個單字或短語是否插入語，例如 however。如果插入語不太妨礙句子的行文，寫作時大可省略逗號。但無論對句子行文的影響如何，也絕不可省略一個而保留另一個。下面兩句中的標點是不可接受的。

Marjorie's husband, Colonel Nelson paid us a visit yesterday.

馬祖利的丈夫克隆尼・尼爾遜，昨天來到我們家。

My brother you will be pleased to hear, is now in perfect health.

告訴你一個好消息，我哥哥現在身體非常好。

根據此規則，非限制性關係從句，也應該由逗號分隔開。

The audience, which had at first been indifferent, became more and more interested.

觀眾一開始反應冷淡，後來興致漸濃。

以 where 和 when 引出的類似句子也要以相同方法來標示逗號。

In 1769, when Napoleon was born, Corsica had but recently been acquired by France.

1769 年，即拿破崙出生的時候，法國剛剛買下了科西嘉島。

Nether Stowey, where Coleridge wrote *The Rime of the Ancient Mariner*, is a few miles from Bridgewater.

尼德斯托威，也就是柯勒律治寫下《古舟子詠》的地方，距離布里奇沃特只有數英里。

以上三個由 which 、 when 和 where 引出的分句是非限制性的；他們並不限定其先行詞，而是對主句中的先行詞進行補充說明。每一個句子都是由兩個句子合併而成，可以寫成兩個獨立完整的句子。

The audience was at first indifferent. Later it became more and more interested.

觀眾一開始反應冷淡。後來他們興致漸濃。

Napoleon was born in 1769. At that time Corsica had but recently been acquired by France.

拿破崙出生於 1769 年。那時，法國剛剛買下了科西嘉島。

Coleridge wrote *The Rime of the Ancient Mariner* at Nether Stowey. Nether Stowey is only a few miles from Bridgewater.

柯勒律治在尼德斯托威寫下《古舟子詠》。尼德斯托威距離布里奇沃特只有數英里。

限制性關係從句不用逗號分隔。

The candidate who best meets these requirements will obtain the place.

符合這些要求的申請人將可獲得這個職位。

在這句話中，限制性關係從句界定了 candidate 這個字所指的對象，即某一個人。與上面三句例句不同，此句不能斷開成兩個獨立的句子。

etc. 和 jr. 等縮寫字之前必須使用逗號。除非被用在句末，否則之後也需要使用逗號。

上面提到插入語前後要加上逗號；同樣，主句前面或後面的短語或從屬分句，也要用逗號分隔開。本節及規則四、五、六、七、十六和十八中所舉的例句，應該足以提供詳盡的指引。

如果插入語前面有連詞，則將第一個逗號寫在連詞之前，而不是之後。

He saw us coming, and unaware that we had learned of his treachery, greeted us with a smile.

他看到我們走近，沒有察覺我們已經知道他背叛的事，依然笑臉相迎。

4. 以連詞 and 或 but 引出獨立分句，要在 and 或 but 前標示逗號

The early records of the city have disappeared, and the story of its first years can no longer be reconstructed.

這座城市早期的記錄已經失去，早年的事蹟已無從考證。

The situation is perilous, but there is still one chance of escape.

形勢十分危急，但仍然有逃脫的機會。

若撇除語境，這類句子似乎需要重寫。到第一個分句的逗號時，句子的意思已經清楚明白，所以第二個分句有點像事後補充的想法。再者，and 是連接詞中最模棱兩可的。如果在獨立分句之間用 and，只是指明兩句有關係，但沒指明是甚麼關係。上述例句中，兩句的關係是因果關係，因此可以改寫成：

As the early records of the city have disappeared, the story of its first years can no longer be reconstructed.

由於這座城市早期的記錄已經失去，早年的事蹟已無從考證。

Although the situation is perilous, there is still one chance of escape.

雖然形勢十分危急，但仍然有逃脫的機會。

上述從句也可以用下列短語代替：

Owing to the disappearance of the early records of the city, the story of its first years can no longer be reconstructed.

由於這座城市早期的記錄已經失去，早年的事蹟已無從考證。

In this perilous situation, there is still one chance of escape.

在這種危急的情況之下，仍然有逃脱的機會。

可是，寫作時可能會誤將句子寫得太緊湊和單一，或者都變成重點落在句末的掉尾句*。其實，間中加一些結構鬆散的句子，可以令文體不會過於正式，也可讓讀者有喘口氣的機會。因此，前面提到的這類結構鬆散的句子，常出現在輕鬆、非學術類的文章中。不過寫作時要注意，不要濫用這類句子。（見規則十四）。

如果句子由兩部份組成，且第二部份由 as（「因為」的意思）、for、or、nor 和 while（意指 and at the same time，即「同時」）等引出，需要在連詞前加上逗號。

如果兩個獨立分句之間，即第二個獨立分句之前，有另外一個從句，或一個需要用逗號分隔的引導短語，則連詞後不用加逗號。

The situation is perilous, but if we are prepared to act promptly, there is still one chance of escape.

形勢十分危急，但如果我們準備好隨時行動，仍然有逃脱的機會。

由副詞連接的兩個獨立分句的標點，請見下一節。

---

* 掉尾句（Periodic Sentence）指的是將句子的次要成份提前，而將主句或句子的主要意思放置在句末的一種較為正式的書面句型。其特點是設置懸念，強調主句。

不要用逗號直接連接獨立分句

如果兩個或以上的分句語法完整，且中間沒有連詞連接，可組成複合句，宜用分號分隔。

Stevenson's romances are entertaining; they are full of exciting adventures.

史蒂文森的傳奇小說引人入勝；充滿刺激的歷險故事。

It is nearly half past five; we cannot reach town before dark.

差不多五點半了；我們來不及在天黑前到達城鎮了。

上述例句如果各分成兩句，用句號代替分號也是正確的用法。

Stevenson's romances are entertaining. They are full of exciting adventures.

史蒂文森的傳奇小說引人入勝。裏面充滿刺激的歷險故事。

It is nearly half past five. We cannot reach town before dark.

差不多五點半了。我們來不及在天黑前到達城鎮了。

如果加入連詞，則應使用逗號（規則四）。

Stevenson's romances are entertaining, for they are full of exciting adventures.

史蒂文森的傳奇小説引人入勝，因為充滿刺激的歷險故事。

It is nearly half past five, and we cannot reach town before dark.

差不多五點半了，我們來不及在天黑前到達城鎮了。

注意，如果第二個分句前面有副詞，如 accordingly、besides、so、then、therefore 或 thus，而不是連詞，則仍需使用分號。

I had never been in the place before; so I had difficulty in finding my way about.

我從來沒到過那裏；所以找路對我來説很困難。

一般來説，最好在寫作中避免以這種方式使用 so，因為作者很可能會用得過於頻繁。一個簡單而行之有效的方法就是刪去 so，用 as 開始新分句：

As I had never been in the place before, I had difficulty in finding my way about.

由於我從來沒到過那裏，找路對我來説很困難。

如果分句很短，而且形式相似，通常也可以用逗號：

Man proposes, God disposes.

謀事在人，成事在天。

The gate swung apart, the bridge fell, the portcullis was drawn up.

大門晃來晃去，橋塌下來，吊閘被拉上去。

6. 不要將一個完整的句子拆成兩句

換句話說，不要用句號代替逗號。

I met them on a Cunard liner several years ago. Coming home from Liverpool to New York.

我和他們是幾年前在利物浦開往紐約的冠達郵輪上認識的。

He was an interesting talker. A man who had traveled all over the world and lived in half a dozen countries.

他談話生動有趣，曾到世界各地旅行，還在六個國家居住過。

以上例句中，第一個句號應用逗號代替，並將後面那個字的第一個字母小寫。

可以將需要強調的字詞或短語變成句子，並加上適當的標點符號：

Again and again he called out. No reply.

他一次又一次地打電話。無人接聽。

不過，寫作時要確定這樣的強調是必要的，而且不要令人誤以為這只是標點符號出錯。

規則三、四、五、六涵蓋了普通句子中，標點符號使用的最重要法則。作者必須精通這些法則，並運用自如。

句首的分詞短語所指涉的主語要和主句主語保持一致

Walking slowly down the road, he saw a woman accompanied by two children.

他在路上慢步徐行，看到一個帶着兩個小孩的女人。

walking 的主語，指的是主句的主語 he，而不是 woman。如果要指 woman，則句子需要改寫成：

He saw a woman accompanied by two children, walking slowly down the road.

他看到一個帶着兩個小孩的女人在路上慢步徐行。

由連詞或介詞引出的分詞短語、名詞同位語、形容詞或形容詞短語，如果位於句首，也需遵循同樣的規則。

* On arriving in Chicago, his friends met him at the station.

When he arrived (or, On his arrival) in Chicago, his friends met him at the station.

他到達芝加哥時，朋友在車站迎接他。

---

* 表示作者不建議的用法。

* A soldier of proved valor, they entrusted him with the defence of the city.

A soldier of proved valor, he was entrusted with the defence of the city.

身為一名英勇的士兵，他獲委以守衛這座城的重任。

* Young and inexperienced, the task seemed easy to me.

Young and inexperienced, I thought the task easy.

我當時年輕又缺乏經驗，以為這項任務很容易完成。

* Without a friend to counsel him, the temptation proved irresistible.

Without a friend to counsel him, he found the temptation irresistible.

沒有朋友在一旁給他忠告，他無法抵擋誘惑。

如果沒有運用此規則，句子就會顯得很荒謬：

Being in a dilapidated condition, I was able to buy the house very cheap.

處於破舊不堪的狀態，我用極低的價錢就買到了這個房子。

行末斷字時要遵守字的組成和發音規則

如果句末的空間只能容納一個或兩個音節，而不是整個單字，那麼將字拆開。以下情況請不要拆字：只有一個字母或是較長單字中的兩個字母被分到下一行。這裏沒有唯一的定律。最常用的原則如下：

A. 按字的構成拆解單字：

know-ledge（而不是 knowl-edge）

Shake-speare（而不是 Shakes-peare）

de-scribe（而不是 des-cribe）

atmo-sphere（而不是 atmos-phere）

B. 以元音為界拆解單字：

edi-ble（而不是 ed-ible） propo-sition

ordi-nary espe-cial

reli-gious oppo-nents

regu-lar classi-fi-ca-tion（三種方法都可以）

deco-rative presi-dent

C. 在重疊的字母處分字成節，除非重疊字母出現在單字原型的末尾：

Apen-nines	Cincin-nati
refer-ring	tell-ing

至於連續幾個輔音的拆解方法，最好請參考以下示例：

for-tune	pic-ture
presump-tuous	illus-tration
sub-stan-tial（兩種均可）	indus-try
instruc-tion	sug-ges-tion
incen-diary	

只要選一本印刷嚴謹的書，多看幾頁，學生就會明白音節的拆解方法。

III

英文寫作十大原則

9. 以段落為基礎單位，一段一主題

如果題目範圍不廣，或者只想簡明扼要地處理，就不必分出主題。因此，簡單的描述、文學作品的撮要、簡短地描述一件事、一個活動和想法，最好都用一個段落解決。寫完之後，再推敲一下是否分主題寫會更好。

不過，通常一個主題需要分成小主題，作為每個段落的主旨。目的當然是為了幫助讀者理解。每一段落的首句都向讀者表明，主題發展已經進入了一個新的階段。

主題的劃分要視乎文章的長短。例如，書或詩歌的短評可能只有一段，而略微長一點的文章可能有兩段。

A. 作品簡介

B. 相關評論

文學課要寫詩詞賞析時，可以分為七段描述：

A. 作品資料及出版資訊

B. 詩體與詩韻格式

C. 主題

D. 表現主題的手法

E. 賞評要點

F. 詩人特色

G. 與其他作品的關係

C 段和 D 段的內容會因詩而異。C 段通常會交代詩中真實的或虛構的場景，如需進一步闡釋，就會點明主題，再勾勒情節的發展。如果全詩以第三人稱敍述，C 段只需要撮寫出情節即可。D 段則點出詩歌所傳達的主要思想，並指出這些意念是如何突顯出來的，或者指出作者主要強調的要點。

若評論小說，則可以從以下主題來討論：

A. 場景設定

B. 情節描述

C. 角色介紹

D. 故事主旨

評論歷史事件，可以從以下主題來着手討論：

A. 事件起因

B. 事件內容

C. 事件影響

撰寫以上這兩類文章時，作者可能需要將上述某些主題再細分成若干小主題。

原則上說，應避免將單一句子單獨成段。但如果是轉折語氣的句子，用來指出上下文的說明或論證的關係時，單一句子也不妨自成一段。

在對話中，每一句話，就算只有一個單字，也能自成一段；每當說話的人改變，都要另起新段。至於如何在對話和敘述結合的文體中應用此規則，最好的方法是以排版嚴謹的小說來作為學習的範例。

10. 每段以主題句開始，段尾要與段首呼應

這樣做的目的也是為了幫助讀者理解。這裏所建議的方法使讀者一開始便能掌握各段主旨，一邊閱讀一邊留下印象，直至最後。因此，最有助於讀者理解的段落，特別是在說明文和議論文當中，應該是這樣的：

A. 主題句位於段首或接近段首的位置；

B. 闡釋、支持或拓展主題句的句子緊隨其後；

C. 最後一句用來強調主題或陳述某些重要的後果。

特別要避免結尾時離題，或者談及無關緊要的細節。

假如該段落處於較長的文章之中，則可能需要指出該段與上文的關聯，或者該段在全文中的作用。有時僅在主題句中加入 again、therefore、for the same reason 之類的單字或短語即可。有時候，也可以在主題句前加一句或幾句介紹性的句子或過渡句。但如果這類句子不止一句，最好將他們獨立成段。

如上所述，作者可以根據寫作目的，用一種或多種方式來連接主題句與段落的內容。為了更清晰地表達主題句，作者可以用其他方式重申主題句，定義當中的某些字詞，善用駁論及舉例論

證；也可以用論據支持主題句，或者進一步說明主題觀點的含意和影響。撰寫較長的段落時，作者可同時運用以上幾種方法。

1. Now, to be properly enjoyed, a walking tour should be gone upon alone.

   主題句。

2. If you go in a company, or even in pairs, it is no longer a walking tour in anything but name; it is something else and more in the nature of a picnic.

   否定相反觀點，使主題更清晰。

3. A walking tour should be gone upon alone, because freedom is of the essence; because you should be able to stop and go on, and follow this way or that, as the freak takes you; and because you must have your own pace, and neither trot alongside a champion walker, nor mince in time with a girl.

   以簡要的方式重複主題句，然後列出三個理由證明；第三個理由（你必須有自己的步伐節奏）通過否定相反觀點，令表達的意思更清晰。

4. And you must be open to all impressions and let your thoughts take colour from what you see.

   以兩種方式表達第四個理由。

5. You should be as a pipe for any wind to play upon.

   理由同上，但是用另一種方式表示。

6. "I cannot see the wit," says Hazlitt, "of walking and talking at the same time."

理由同上，引用黑玆利特的説法。

7. When I am in the country, I wish to vegetate like the country, which is the gist of all that can be said upon the matter.

   理由同上，引用黑玆利特的説法。

8. There should be no cackle of voices at your elbow, to jar on the meditative silence of the morning.

   用稍為不同的字句，重複黑玆利特的理由。

9. And so long as a man is reasoning he cannot surrender himself to that fine intoxication that comes of much motion in the open air, that begins in a sort of dazzle and sluggishness of the brain, and ends in a peace that passes comprehension. – Stevenson, *Walking Tours*.

   最後一次重申第四個理由，但用詞和語氣更強烈，令結論強而有力。

1. It was chiefly in the eighteenth century that a very different conception of history grew up.

   主題句。

2. Historians then came to believe that their task was not so much to paint a picture as to solve a problem; to explain or illustrate the successive phases of national growth, prosperity, and adversity.

   使主題句更清晰；為新歷史觀下定義。

3. The history of morals, of industry, of intellect, and of art; the changes that take place in manners or beliefs; the dominant ideas that prevailed in successive periods; the rise, fall, and modification of political constitutions; in a word, all the conditions of national well-being became the subject of their works.

   拓展定義。

4. They sought rather to write a history of peoples than a history of kings.

   用對比闡釋定義。

5. They looked especially in history for the chain of causes and effects.

   補充定義：提出新歷史觀的另一個元素。

6. They undertook to study in the past the physiology of nations, and hoped by applying the experimental method on a large scale to deduce some lessons of real value about the conditions on which the welfare of society mainly depend. – Lecky, *The Political Value of History*.

   結論：新歷史觀的重要影響。

記敍性和描寫性的段落，有時會用一句結構精簡、意思全面的句子開始，總括後面的細節。

The breeze served us admirably.
微風徐徐吹來，美好極了。

The campaign opened with a series of reverses.
這場運動一開始就連番受挫。

The next ten or twelve pages were filled with a curious set of entries.

接下來的十到十二頁列出一些稀奇古怪的詞條。

但是，這種方法如果用得太濫，就會變得矯揉造作。更常見的做法，是僅在首句點出該段的主要內容即可。

At length I thought I might return towards the stockade.

最終，我覺得自己還是會回到城寨裏去。

He picked up the heavy lamp from the table and began to explore.

他從桌子上提起那盞很重的燈，便開始四處探索。

Another flight of steps, and they emerged on the roof.

他們再爬了幾段階梯，就來到了屋頂。

不過，描述生動的敍述性段落，通常較為簡短且沒有主題句。這些段落之間的不連貫，具有修辭上的停頓作用，可以突顯某些情節中的細節。

11. 使用主動語態

主動語態通常比被動語態更直接、更有力：

> I shall always remember my first visit to Boston.
> 我會永遠記得第一次去波士頓的經歷。

此句比下面的例句要好很多：

> My first visit to Boston will always be remembered by me.
> 第一次去波士頓的經歷，會讓我永遠記得。

第二句不夠直接、大膽和簡潔，如果作者為了精簡而刪去「by me」：

> My first visit to Boston will always be remembered.
> 我第一次去波士頓的經歷，將會永遠被記得。

句子就會變得含糊：到底是誰會記得這次經歷，是作者、某位身份不明的人士，還是全世界？

當然，這項規則不是指作者必須完全摒棄被動語態；很多時候被動語態還是很方便且必要的。

The dramatists of the Restoration are little esteemed today.

復興時期的劇作家現在不再受到重視。

Modern readers have little esteem for the dramatists of the Restoration.

現代讀者幾乎不重視復興時期的劇作家 。

第一句用在論述復興時期的劇作家的段落中為好，而第二句則用在描述現代讀者的鑒賞力的段落中為宜。如上述例句所示，選用哪個字詞作為句子的主語，常常決定了要使用哪一種語態。

然而，使用主動語態可以使文字更有說服力。此規則不僅適用於有大量情節描寫的記敍文，也適用於任何文體。很多時候，只要採用及物動詞的主動語態來代替 there is 或 could be heard 等泛泛而談之詞，則原本平淡無奇的描寫和說明性的文字就會立刻變得生動起來，重點突出。

* There were a great number of dead leaves lying on the ground.

地上有很多落葉。

Dead leaves covered the ground.

落葉鋪滿一地。

* The sound of the falls could still be heard.

瀑布的聲響還聽得到。

The sound of the falls still reached our ears.

瀑布的響聲仍然在耳邊迴響。

* The reason that he left college was that his health became impaired.

他離校是因為健康出了問題。

Failing health compelled him to leave college.

健康問題使他不得不離開學校。

* It was not long before he was very sorry that he had said what he had.

很快他就為自己的話感到非常抱歉。

He soon repented his words.

他很快就後悔說了那些話。

原則上說，不要將一個被動句疊加到另一個被動句上。

* Gold was not allowed to be exported.

It was forbidden to export gold (The export of gold was prohibited).

以前出口黃金是不被允許的。

* He has been proved to have been seen entering the building.

It has been proved that he was seen to enter the building.

有證據顯示他被目擊進入過那幢大樓。

上面兩個例句在修改之前，與第二個被動動作相關的字詞同時也是第一個被動動作的主語。

另一個寫作的通病，就是用一個名詞作為被動動作的主語，代表了整個動作，令動詞除了完整句子結構外毫無用處。

* A survey of this region was made in 1900.
1900 年的時候有人考察過這個地區。

This region was surveyed in 1900.
這個地區在 1900 年時有人考察過。

* Mobilization of the army was rapidly effected.
軍隊動員十分迅速。

The army was rapidly mobilized.
軍隊被迅速地調動起來。

* Confirmation of these reports cannot be obtained.
這些報告內容的確認無法獲得。

These reports cannot be confirmed.
這些報告的內容不能獲得確認。

相較之下，例句「The export of gold was prohibited.」的謂語「was prohibited」就表達出了「export」沒有的意思。

12. 用肯定句陳述

主張要明確。避免平淡乏味、含混不清、不置可否的表達。用 not 表示否定或對立的概念，而不是用作遁辭。

* He was not very often on time.
以前他不總是那樣準時。

He usually came late.
以前他總是遲到。

* He did not think that studying Latin was much use.
以前他不覺得學拉丁文有甚麼用。

He thought the study of Latin useless.
以前他覺得學拉丁文沒有用。

* *The Taming of the Shrew* is rather weak in spots. Shakespeare does not portray Katharine as a very admirable character, nor does Bianca remain long in memory as an important character in Shakespeare's works.
《馴悍記》在某些地方比較薄弱。莎士比亞沒有將凱瑟琳塑造成一個令人欽佩的角色，碧安卡也不可能作為莎劇中的一個重要人物而長留在人們的記憶中。

The women in *The Taming of the Shrew* are unattractive. Katharine is disagreeable, Bianca insignificant.

《馴悍記》的女角都不大吸引人。凱瑟琳不討人喜歡，碧安卡則顯得無足輕重。

最後一例在修改前使用了否定句式，意思不夠明確。因此，修正後的版本只能是對作者原意的猜測。

以上三句都表明 not 這個字眼內在的弱點。不管有沒有意識到，讀者並不滿足於被告知「不是甚麼」，而是更想知道到底「是甚麼」。因此，一般來說，即使是否定的意思，也最好用肯定的形式來表達。

not honest 不誠實
dishonest 欺詐

not important 不重要
trifling 微不足道

did not remember 不記得
forgot 遺忘

did not pay any attention to 沒有留意
ignored 忽略

did not have much confidence in 沒有信心
distrusted 不信任

否定與肯定的對比效果非常強烈：

Not charity, but simple justice.
不是為了做善事，只是為了討回公道。

Not that I loved Caesar less, but Rome the more.
我不是不愛凱撒，只是更愛羅馬。

除 not 以外的否定字眼通常語氣強烈：

The sun never sets upon the British flag.
照耀着英國旗的太陽永遠不會落下。

13. 刪去贅字

生動有力的表達是精煉的。句中不應有冗詞，正如段中不應有贅句。同樣，圖畫不應有多餘線條，機器也不應有多餘零件。要做到精煉，不是要求作者裁短每個句子或者略去每個細節，只勾勒出主題的輪廓；而是要求每一個字都必須表情達意。

很多常見的用語都違反了此規則：

* the question as to whether
關於到底……這個問題

whether (the question whether)
到底（到底……這個問題）

* there is no doubt but that
毋庸置疑的是

no doubt (doubtless)
毋庸置疑

* used for fuel purposes
用作燃料之用

used for fuel
用作燃料

* he is a man who
他是一個……的人

he
他……

* in a hasty manner
以匆忙的方式

hastily
匆忙地

* this is a subject which
這是一個……的題材

this subject
這題材……

* His story is a strange one.
他的故事是一個很奇特的故事

His story is strange.
他的故事很奇特。

特別是 the fact that 這個短語，應該從每一句中剔除。

* owing to the fact that
基於……的事實

since (because)
由於、因為

* in spite of the fact that
儘管有……的事實

though (although)
雖然

* call your attention to the fact that
令你注意……的事實

remind you (notify you)
提醒你

* I was unaware of the fact that
我不知道有……的事實

I was unaware that (did not know)
我不知道

* the fact that he had not succeeded
他沒有成功的這個事實

his failure
他的失敗

* the fact that I had arrived
我已到來的這個事實

my arrival

我的到來

參見第五章中 case、character、nature、system 的用法。

通常 who is、which was 之類的字詞是多餘的。

* His brother, who is a member of the same firm

His brother, a member of the same firm

他的哥哥，也是同一家公司的成員

* Trafalgar, which was Nelson's last battle

Trafalgar, Nelson's last battle

特拉法之役，即尼爾遜將軍的最後一戰

肯定句比否定句精簡，主動語態又比被動語態精煉。許多規則 11 和 12 中舉出的例子，也證實了這條精簡原則。

有一個違反精簡原則的通病，就是按部就班地表達一個複雜的概念，原本可以用一句話表達的，卻用了一連串句子。

* Macbeth was very ambitious. This led him to wish to become king of Scotland. The witches told him that this wish of his would come true. The king of Scotland at this time was Duncan. Encouraged by his wife, Macbeth murdered Duncan. He was thus enabled to succeed Duncan as king. (55 words.)

馬克白很有野心。這性格使他有了當蘇格蘭國王的念頭。

眾女巫告訴他，他的願望最終會實現。當時蘇格蘭國王是鄧肯。在妻子鼓勵下，馬克白殺掉鄧肯。於是他成功登上蘇格蘭國王的寶座。

Encouraged by his wife, Macbeth achieved his ambition and realized the prediction of the witches by murdering Duncan and becoming king of Scotland in his place. (26 words.)

在妻子鼓勵下，馬克白成功實現了他的野心，也證實了女巫說他會殺掉鄧肯，繼而登上蘇格蘭國王寶座的預言。

14. 避免使用一連串結構鬆散的句子

此原則適用於某一類的結構鬆散的句子，即由兩個並列分句組成，當中第二句以連詞或關係詞引出的句子。儘管這一類句子單獨使用時無可厚非（見規則四），但連續使用難免會單調乏味。

文筆欠佳的作者有時會寫上整段這樣的句子，主要用連詞 and、but，其次是非限制性意義的關係詞，例如 who、which、when、where、while（見規則三）。

The third concert of the subscription series was given last evening, and a large audience was in attendance. Mr. Edward Appleton was the soloist, and the Boston Symphony Orchestra furnished the instrumental music. The former showed himself to be an artist of the first rank, while the latter proved itself fully deserving of its high reputation. The interest aroused by the series has been very gratifying to the Committee, and it is planned to give a similar series annually hereafter. The fourth concert will be given on Tuesday, May 10, when an equally attractive programme will be presented.

第三場慈善音樂會於昨晚舉行，出席人數眾多。由愛德華・阿普頓先生擔任獨唱，配樂部份由波士頓管弦樂團演奏。前者演出水準一流，後者亦名不虛傳。本系列廣受好評，委員會也很高興，正在籌劃每一年將繼續舉辦類似的系列演出。第四場演唱會將於 5 月 10 日星期二舉行，屆時同樣會有精彩的節目。

除了行文顯得造作、空泛外，這段文字的欠缺之處還在於其句子結構千篇一律，節奏單調乏味。拿這一段和規則十的例句比較一下，或者和任何一篇英文佳作，例如《浮華世界》的序言（Before the Curtain）比較。

假如作者發現自己已經寫了一系列結構鬆散的句子，那他必須重寫相當一部份以避免語言過於單調。他可以寫一些簡單句，用分號連接的兩個分句，兩個分句組成的掉尾句，三個分句組成的鬆散句或掉尾句 —— 一定要改寫成能夠準確表達文章思路之間邏輯關係的句子。

使用相似的句型結構表達對等的概念

平行結構這個原則，要求意思相近，功能相似的概念，在結構上也要類似。結構相似，令讀者一眼看清句子內容和功能的相近之處。常見的例子包括《聖經》中的十誡、天國八福和主禱文。

文筆不佳的作者常常違反此規則，誤以為要經常轉變表達方式。有時候為了強調而重複語意，的確需要改變句子的結構。詳見規則十裏史蒂文森的例子。除此之外，他必須要遵守平行結構的原則。

* Formerly, science was taught by the textbook method, while now the laboratory method is employed.

以前，科學知識採用教科書的方式教授，現在卻用實驗的方式。

Formerly, science was taught by the textbook method; now it is taught by the laboratory method.

以前，科學知識採用教科書的方式教授，而現在的科學知識則是通過實驗的方式傳授。

上句令人覺得作者猶疑不決、畏首畏尾，好像不敢決定和貫徹某一種表達方式。下句則顯示作者最終決定了用一種結構，而且貫徹始終。

根據此規則，適用於一組短語的冠詞或介詞，必須只在第一個字詞前使用，或須每個字詞前都要重複。

* The French, the Italians, Spanish, and Portuguese

The French, the Italians, the Spanish, and the Portuguese

法國人、意大利人、西班牙人、葡萄牙人

* In spring, summer, or in winter

In spring, summer, or winter (In spring, in summer, or in winter)

春天、夏天、或者冬天裏

相關連接詞（both、and；not、but；not only、but also；either、or；first、second、third 等等）後的詞組要有相同的文法結構。很多違反了此規則的句子可以通過重組句子的結構來修正。

* It was both a long ceremony and very tedious.

The ceremony was both long and tedious.

這個典禮既冗長又乏味。

* A time not for words, but action.

A time not for words, but for action.

坐言不如起行。

* Either you must grant his request or incur his ill will.

You must either grant his request or incur his ill will.

要不你允許他的請求，要不就得忍受他的怨恨。

* My objections are, first, the injustice of the measure; second, that it is unconstitutional.

My objections are, first, that the measure is unjust; second, that it is unconstitutional.

我反對的理由是，第一，這提案不符合公義；第二，它不符合憲法。

另見規則十二例三，以及規則十三最後一例。

可能有人會問：如果作者想表達很多意思相近的概念呢，比如二十個？必須連續寫二十個結構相同的句子嗎？仔細想想，不難發現這個問題是不存在的，因為這二十個概念可以歸類分組，然後在各組別裏應用此規則即可。不然，他最好使用圖表，避免碰到上述的問題。

16. 相關的字詞要放在一起

字詞在句子中的位置，是表示字與字之間相互關係的主要手段。因此，作者必須盡量將意思相關的字詞及詞組放在一起，將不那麼相干的字詞隔開。

原則上說，句子的主語和主要動詞不應被可移到句首的短語或分句隔開。

* Wordsworth, in the fifth book of *The Excursion*, gives a minute description of this church.

In the fifth book of *The Excursion*, Wordsworth gives a minute description of this church.

在《漫遊》的第五本中，華茲華斯細緻地描繪了這座教堂。

* Cast iron, when treated in a Bessemer converter, is changed into steel.

By treatment in a Bessemer converter, cast iron is changed into steel.

通過貝塞麥轉爐法將鑄鐵煉製成鋼。

反對理由是，插入的短語或分句毫無必要地打斷了主句的自然語序。不過，這條理由通常不適用於由關係從句或同位語構成的插入短語，也不適用於掉尾句，後者是為了製造懸念而故意使用插入語的。（例子請參見規則十八）

關係代詞原則上必須緊隨先行詞之後。

* There was a look in his eye that boded mischief.

In his eye was a look that boded mischief.

他眼中流露出頑皮的神情。

* He wrote three articles about his adventures in Spain, which were published in *Harper's Magazine*.

He published in *Harper's Magazine* three articles about his adventures in Spain.

他在《哈潑雜誌》上刊登了三篇自己在西班牙歷險的文章。

* This is a portrait of Benjamin Harrison, grandson of William Henry Harrison, who became President in 1889.

This is a portrait of Benjamin Harrison, grandson of William Henry Harrison. He became President in 1889.

這是班哲明・哈里森的肖像，他是威廉・亨利・哈里森的孫兒。他在 1889 年成為總統。

如果先行詞由一組字詞構成，則將關係代詞放在詞組的最後，除非這樣做會引起歧義。

The Superintendent of the Chicago Division, who
芝加哥分會的負責人，即……

* A proposal to amend the Sherman Act, which has been variously judged.

A proposal, which has been variously judged, to amend the Sherman Act

提出修訂謝爾曼法這項倍受爭議的動議……

A proposal to amend the much-debated Sherman Act
一項提出修訂倍受爭議之謝爾曼法的動議……

* The grandson of William Henry Harrison, who

William Henry Harrison's grandson, Benjamin Harrison, who

威廉・亨利・哈里森的孫兒，班哲明・哈里森，他……

同位語名詞可以夾在先行詞和關係代詞之間，因為這樣的結構不會產生歧義。

The Duke of York, his brother, who was regarded with hostility by the Whigs

約克公爵，也就是他的兄弟，遭到輝格黨的針對

修飾語應該盡可能靠近被修飾的對象。如果同一個字有幾個修飾語，必須小心安排它們的次序，以免令讀者錯誤解讀修飾關係。

* All the members were not present.

Not all the members were present.

不是所有成員都出席了。

* He only found two mistakes.

He found only two mistakes.

他發現只有兩個錯處。

* Major R. E. Joyce will give a lecture on Tuesday evening in Bailey Hall, to which the public is invited, on "My Experiences in Mesopotamia" at eight P. M.

On Tuesday evening at eight P. M., Major R. E. Joyce will give in Bailey Hall a lecture on "My Experiences in Mesopotamia." The public is invited.

星期二晚上八時，喬斯少校將在貝里廳舉行分享會，題為「我在美索不達米亞的經歷」，歡迎公眾參加。

17. 用同一種時態寫撮要

撰寫劇本的撮要時，作者應該使用現在時態。詩歌、故事和小說的撮要，也最好使用現在時態。當然，如果作者喜歡，用過去時態亦無不可。如果情節撮要是用現在時態寫成，則之前的情節應該使用現在完成時態；如果是以過去時態寫成，則之前的情節應該使用過去完成時態。

> An unforeseen chance prevents Friar John from delivering Friar Lawrence's letter to Romeo. Juliet, meanwhile, owing to her father's arbitrary change of the day set for her wedding, has been compelled to drink the potion on Tuesday night, with the result that Balthasar informs Romeo of her supposed death before Friar Lawrence learns of the nondelivery of the letter.

> 一個始料不及的意外，使修道士約翰未能將修道士勞倫斯的信交給羅密歐。與此同時，由於茱麗葉的父親臨時改動了她的婚期，她不得以在星期二晚上就喝下了麻醉藥。結果，在修道士勞倫斯知悉信還沒有送達給羅密歐之前，巴爾塔隆已經將朱麗葉所謂的死訊告訴了羅密歐。

不過，無論情節撮要是使用哪種時態，間接引語和間接疑問句中的過去時態應該保持不變。

The Legate inquires who struck the blow.
教皇使節詢問是誰先發的難。

除了上述的例外情況，無論作者選用哪一種時態，都應該貫徹始終。經常轉換時態會予人猶疑不定、優柔寡斷之感（比較規則十五）。

陳述他人的觀點和意見時，比如撰寫論文的撮要、轉述別人的話語，作者應避免插入以下用語：「he said」、「he stated」、「the speaker added」、「the speaker then went on to say」、「the author also thinks」以及類似的表達方式。作者應該在一開始就一次交代清楚後面只是撮要敍述，之後就不必贅言重複。

在筆記、報章、文學手冊裏，各種撮寫是不可或缺的。對於小學學童，撮寫可以幫助他們用自己的話語重新敍述一個故事。但在寫文學評論或詮釋時，作者必須小心，避免寫成了撮寫。他可能覺得有必要用一兩句撮寫來指明主題或開場的情景，也可能列出大量細節來表現作品的特點。然而，作者應該在文中條理分明地提出論點及論據，而不是撮寫情節大綱，偶然加幾筆評語。同樣，如果論述的範圍涉及多部作品，作者不應按年份逐一論述，而應該從一開始就致力於確立總的結論。一般來說，這樣可以寫得更好。

18. 強調的字眼要放在句末

作者最想強調的單字或詞組，最適合放在句末。

* Humanity has hardly advanced in fortitude since that time, though it has advanced in many other ways.

從那時候開始人性就沒有變得更剛強，雖然在其他方面倒進步不少。

Humanity, since that time, has advanced in many other ways, but it has hardly advanced in fortitude.

人性從那時候開始在各方面都有進步，卻沒有變得更剛強。

* This steel is principally used for making razors, because of its hardness.

這種鋼主要用來製造剃刀，因為它夠堅硬。

Because of its hardness, this steel is principally used in making razors.

因為這種鋼夠堅硬，所以主要用來製造剃刀。

適合放在這個重要位置的單字或詞組，通常是邏輯謂語，也就是句子中提供新資訊的部份，正如上面第二個例句所示。

掉尾句的效果，便是通過這種對主要陳述的強調而得來。

Four centuries ago, Christopher Columbus, one of the Italian mariners whom the decline of their own republics had put at the service of the world and of adventure, seeking for Spain a westward passage to the Indies as a set-off against the achievements of Portuguese discoverers, lighted on America.

四個世紀前，克利斯托夫・哥倫布，一位意大利航海家，因國內共和體制衰亡而從事探索世界的冒險航行；在為西班牙尋找一條通向印度群島的西行航線，以抵消葡萄牙探險家的成就時，偶然發現了美洲。

With these hopes and in this belief I would urge you, laying aside all hindrance, thrusting away all private aims, to devote yourself unswervingly and unflinchingly to the vigorous and successful prosecution of this war.

滿懷希望和信念，我在此呼籲各位，排除所有障礙，拋開一切私念，堅定不移、毫不畏縮地投入這場轟烈的戰爭裏，直至得勝。

另一個有強調作用的位置是句首。句中除主語外的任何成份，只要置於句首，都會變得更顯著。

Deceit or treachery he could never forgive.

欺詐和背叛是他決不會原諒的行為。

So vast and rude, fretted by the action of nearly three thousand years, the fragments of this architecture may often seem, at first sight, like works of nature.

這座建築物龐大而簡陋的斷壁殘垣，在歷經近三千年的磨蝕後，第一眼看去就像大自然的作品。

主語放在句首可以起強調之用，但這往往不單是因為位置關係。例如下句：

> Great kings worshipped at his shrine.
> 偉大的君主在他的神龕前敬拜。

kings 之所以受到強調，是由於其本身的意思及所處的上下文。要達到特別強調的效果，句子主語必須安置在謂語的位置。

> Through the middle of the valley flowed a winding stream.
> 山谷間出現一道蜿蜒的小溪。

將強調字眼放在句末的規則，可應用於多個層面，包括句子中的字詞，段落中的句子，以及文章中的段落。

IV

格式注意事項

1. 標題

標題或原稿題目後留一空行，或大約一行的空位。在隨後的頁面上，如果是用有間隔線的紙，應從第一行開始書寫。

2. 數字

日期或其他序數不需要拼寫出來。用阿拉伯數字或羅馬數字表示即可。

August 9, 1918
1918 年 8 月 9 日

Rule 3
第 3 條

Chapter XII
第 12 章

352d Infantry
步兵 352 師

3. 圓括號

句中有括號夾注的詞句時，其加標點的方式如下：對於圓括號外的語言，其標點符號的處理，如同括號不存在時一樣；對於圓括號內的語言，要按其意思加標點，但最後的句號要省略，而問號和感嘆號則需保留。

I went to his house yesterday (my third attempt to see him), but he had left town.

昨天我去他家（已經是第三次去找他），但他出城去了。

He declares (and why should we doubt his good faith?) that he is now certain of success.

他宣稱（我們又何必懷疑他的信念？）他確信自己會成功。

（如果括號夾注的是一個完整獨立的短語或句子，最後的句號要放在後面的那個圓括號之前。）

4. 引文

作為書面證明的正式的引文，應用冒號引出，然後加上前後引號。

The provision of the Constitution is: "No tax or duty shall be laid on articles exported from any state."

憲法寫明：「不准向任何州份的出口貨品徵稅。」

如果引文在語法上是同位語或動詞的直接賓語，應在前面加上逗號，然後加上前後引號。

I recall the maxim of La Rochefoucauld, "Gratitude is a lively sense of benefits to come."

我想起拉羅什富科的座右銘：「感恩就是對日後回報的追求。」

Aristotle says, "Art is an imitation of nature."

亞里士多德説：「藝術是對大自然的模仿。」

引用一整行或多行詩句時，應另開一行並置中，不需加上前後引號。

Wordsworth's enthusiasm for the Revolution was at first unbounded:

華茲華斯對革命的熱情一開始是毫不掩飾的：

> Bliss was it in that dawn to be alive,
> But to be young was very heaven!
> 能活在那個黎明，已是幸福，
> 黎明時正值風華，更是極樂般的欣喜！

以 that 引出的引文視為間接引語，不需要使用引號。

Keats declares that beauty is truth, truth beauty.

濟慈説，美即是真，真即是美。

諺語和人們熟知的、有文學出處的用語不需要加引號。

These are the times that try men's souls.
這就是試煉人們靈魂的時候。

He lives far from the madding crowd.
他住在遠離塵囂的地方。

同理，口頭語和俚語也不需要加引號。

5. 文獻出處

在需要提供準確的文獻出處的學術著作中，經常出現的書名要用縮寫，再在文末的參考文獻中按字母順序列出全名。一般做法是，文獻資料用括號或腳注形式標明，不要出現在正文當中。記住略去 act、scene、line、book、volume、page 這類字眼，除非僅用其中之一。標點體例如下：

* In the second scene of the third act
第三幕第二場

In III.ii（更好的寫法是，直接用括號夾注 III.ii，並置於句中適當的位置。）

After the killing of Polonius, Hamlet is placed under guard (IV.ii.14).
波洛尼厄斯被殺後，哈姆雷特就被監視起來（第 4 幕，第 2 場，第 14 行）。

2 Samuel i:17–27

《撒母耳記》，下卷，第 1 章，第 17 至 27 節

Othello II.iii.264–267, III.iii.155–161

《奧賽羅》，第 2 幕，第 3 場，第 264 至 267 行；第 3 幕，第三場，第 155 至 161 行。

6. 書名

文學作品的名字，學術上傾向於使用斜體，並且大寫每個字的首字母。編輯和出版商的習慣不盡相同：有的使用斜體，並將每個字的首字母大寫；其他的則使用正體加首字母大寫，引號可有可無。多數情況下，採用斜體表示（手稿則畫上底線），除非有些期刊另行規定。如果書名前用了所有格，則應略去書名開頭的冠詞 A 或者 The。

The Iliad; *the Odyssey*; *As You Like It*; *To a Skylark*; *The Newcomes*; *A Tale of Two Cities*; *Dickens's Tale of Two Cities*.

《伊利亞德》、《奧德賽》、《皆大歡喜》、《致雲雀》、《鈕康氏家》、《雙城記》、狄更斯的《雙城記》。

V

常見誤用字詞和短語

（許多列在這裏的字詞和短語，與其說是拙劣的英文，不如說是不良的文風，常見於草率的英文寫作中。以 Feature 為例，改寫的方式不是替換某一個字或一組字詞，而是將模糊籠統的概述，用明確肯定的陳述表達出來。）

1. All right. 好的、行、沒問題

在常用的口頭語中，作獨立短語使用，如同「Agreed」（同意）或「Go ahead」（鼓勵去做）。最好避免在其他情況下使用。兩字必須分開寫。

2. As good or better than. 一樣好，甚至更好

這種句子必須調整其結構，予以更正。

* My opinion is as good or better than his.

My opinion is as good as his, or better (if not better).

我的意見和他的一樣好，甚至更好。

3. As to whether. 是否

單用 whether 已足夠；另見規則十三。

4. Bid. 吩咐

用不帶 to 的不定式，過去式為 bade。

5. Case. 案件、案例、情況

《牛津簡明英語詞典》將該字解作：「某事發生的例子；事件狀況。」表達這兩個意思時，這個字通常沒有必要出現。

> * In many cases, the rooms were poorly ventilated.
> 在很多情況下，房間都是通風不良的。
>
> Many of the rooms were poorly ventilated.
> 很多房間都是通風不良的。
>
> * It has rarely been the case that any mistake has been made.
> 很少有發生錯誤的情況。
>
> Few mistakes have been made.
> 錯誤很少。

見 Wood 所著的《給作者的建議》第 68 至 71 頁，以及 Quiller-Couch 所著的《寫作的藝術》，第 103 至 106 頁。

6. Certainly. 當然、肯定地

被某些人濫用，正如 very 被濫用一樣。用來強調任何乃至每一句陳述的語氣。這種矯揉造作的用語，在口語中是不恰當的，更不應該出現在書面語中。

7. Character. 特點、性格

通常是多餘的，純粹是冗言贅詞的習慣。

* acts of a hostile character
帶有敵意特徵的舉動

hostile acts
懷有敵意的舉動

8. Claim, vb. 聲稱（動詞）

和作為賓語的名詞連用，表示「聲稱或要求擁有權利」（lay claim to）。明確表示這個意思時，可以和從句連用：「He claimed that he was the sole surviving heir.」（他聲稱自己是唯一的繼承人。）。（但即使在這一句中，用「claimed to be」也會更好。）不可與 declare、maintain 或 charge 互換。

9. Compare. 比較

compare to 用來指出或暗示不同種類事物間的相似之處；而 compare with 主要用來指同類事物間的不同之處。因此，人生被比作一場朝聖之旅、一齣戲劇和一場戰役時，用 compared to 進行比較；美國國會和英國國會的比較用 compare with。巴黎被比作古代雅典時用 compared to，而巴黎和倫敦作比較時用 compare with。

10. Clever. 聰敏

這個字被嚴重濫用；最好只用來表示小事情上的機智。

11. Consider. 認為

解作「相信是」(believe to be) 時，後面不加 as。「I consider him thoroughly competent.」(我覺得他完全可以勝任。) 比較下句：「The lecturer considered Cromwell first as soldier and second as administrator.」(講師認為克倫威爾首先是一名士兵，其次才是執政者。) 當中，considered 指經過審視或討論的意思。

12. Dependable. 可靠的

使用 reliable、trustworthy 即可，不必用 dependable 替代。

13. Due to. 由於

在狀語中被誤用作 through、because of 或 owing to 的替代詞，如：「He lost the first game, due to carelessness.」(他因為粗心，輸了第一場比賽。)。正確的用法是，應該作為謂語或特定名詞的修飾語，例如：「This invention is due to Edison.」(這是愛迪生的發明。)、「losses due to preventable fires」(本可預防的火災所導致的損失)。

14. Effect. 影響

作名詞時，指後果、影響，等同 result；作動詞時，解作使發生、使實現，等於 to bring about、accomplish（有別於 affect，後者解作帶來影響）。

作名詞時，常隨意地使用於描寫時裝、音樂、畫作及其他藝術形式等的輕鬆讀物，如「an Oriental effect」（東方效應）、「effects in pale green」（穿淺綠色衣服的效果）、「very delicate effects」（非常柔和的效果）、「broad effects」（廣泛的影響）、「subtle effects」（微妙的效果）、「a charming effect was produced by」（通過……產生了迷人的效果）。

15. Etc. 等等、諸如此類

不適用於列舉人物。等於 and the rest、and so forth。如果前面列出的一項不具代表性，會令讀者感到疑惑，不理解重要的細節，則不能用這個字。最沒有異議的用法，是表示已全部列出之一連串字詞的最後幾個，或引文最後幾個不重要的字詞。

如果列出項目前出現 such as、for example 等類似字眼，就不可以用 etc.。

16. Fact. 事實

只能用在可以直接確認的事物上，不可以用來判斷事物。比如某一天發生了某件事，或者鉛金屬達到某個溫度會熔化，這些都可以用 fact。但涉及個人意見的句子，如拿破崙是當代最偉大的將軍，或者加州氣候很怡人，即使語氣聽起來多麼堅定，都不是事實。

the fact that 的使用規則，請見規則十三。

17. Factor. 因素

常被濫用；含 factor 的語句往往可以用其他更直接、更地道的字詞取代。

* His superior training was the great factor in his winning the match.
他所接受的優質訓練是他致勝的關鍵因素。

He won the match by being better trained.
他勝出是因為接受了較好的訓練。

* Heavy artillery is becoming an increasingly important factor in deciding battles.
重炮日益成為決定關鍵戰役勝敗的重要因素。

Heavy artillery is playing a constantly larger part in deciding battles.
重炮在關鍵戰役中日益重要。

18. Feature. 特色

也是過度使用的字詞。像 factor，通常對句子的意思毫無增益。

> A feature of the entertainment especially worthy of mention was the singing of Miss A.
>
> 那次文娛表演有個特別值得一提的特色，那就是 A 小姐的歌唱表演。
>
> （同樣的字數不如用來描述 A 小姐唱了甚麼歌，如果表演已經完畢，也可以寫她怎樣唱。）

用作動詞時，不要用帶有宣傳意味的「以……為特色」之意。

19. Fix. 固定

在美國口語中等同 arrange（安排）、prepare（準備）、mend（修理）。書寫時，盡量保持書面語裏的意思，相當於 fasten（繫牢）、make firm（使固定）、immovable（不可移動的）等。

20. He is a man who. 他是……的人

常見的贅詞；詳見規則十三。

* He is a man who is very ambitious.
  他是一個很有野心的人。

  He is very ambitious.
  他很有野心。

* Spain is a country which I have always wanted to visit.
  西班牙是我一直想去的國家。

  I have always wanted to visit Spain.
  我一直想去西班牙。

21. However. 但是、無論如何

等於 nevertheless（然而）時，不可以放在句首或分句之首。

* The roads were almost impassable. However, we at last succeeded in reaching camp.
  那些路幾乎無法通過。不過，我們最後還是順利抵達營地。

  The roads were almost impassable. At last, however, we succeeded in reaching camp.
  那些路幾乎無法通過。不過最後，我們還是順利抵達營地。

如果 however 放在首位，意指無論如何，即 in whatever way 或 to whatever extent。

> However you advise him, he will probably do as he thinks best.
> 無論你怎樣勸說他，他只會按照自己認為最好的方式去做。
>
> However discouraging the prospect, he never lost heart.
> 無論前景怎樣黑暗，他從沒有灰心喪氣。

22. Kind of. 某種、有一點

不要用來取代形容詞和動詞前面的 rather，或者名詞前面的 something like，除非語境一致。保持書面語裏的意思，如「Amber is a kind of fossil resin.」（琥珀是一種樹脂化石。）、「I dislike that kind of notoriety.」（我不喜歡那種名人。）。以上規則也適用於 sort of。

23. Less. 較少

不可誤作 fewer。

> * He had less men than in the previous campaign.
>
> He had fewer men than in the previous campaign.
>
> 比起上一次運動，他手下的人少了。

less 指不可數的「量」，fewer 指可數的「數目」。「His troubles are less than mine.」指「他的麻煩沒有我的大。」。「His troubles are fewer than mine.」指「他的麻煩沒有我的多。」。然而，「The signers of the petition were less than a hundred.」（簽署參加這次行動的人少於一百個。）這樣寫是可以的，因為當中的約數 a hundred 類似集合名詞，而 less 可以指數量或總量較少。

24. Line, along these lines. 方式、方法、手段

line 可以指一連串步驟、行為、思想等，但常被濫用，特別是 along these lines。作者如果想顯得清新、有創意，應完全摒棄這個詞。

* Mr. B. also spoke along the same lines.
B 先生也說了類似的話。

Mr. B. also spoke, to the same effect.
B 先生說的跟我大同小異。

* He is studying along the line of French literature.
他在研讀法國文學方面的東西。

He is studying French literature.
他在研讀法國文學。

25. Literal, literally. 照字面的、直接地

通常誤用於突顯誇張手法或過份強烈的比喻。

*a literal flood of abuse.
確實是一輪辱罵

a flood of abuse.
一輪辱罵

*literally dead with fatigue
真是累死了

almost dead with fatigue (dead tired)
快累死了

26. Lose out. 損失、失敗

原本比 lose 更強烈，但由於用得太普遍，實際上變得沒有那麼強烈了，正如 try out、win out、sign up、register up。out 和 up 可與部份動詞合用，形成慣用語，如 find out、run out、turn out、cheer up、dry up、make up 等。每一個都有別於原本單個動詞的意思。注意 lose out 並不在此列。

27. Most. 最

不要誤作 almost。

* most everybody

almost everybody

幾乎所有人

* most all the time

almost all the time

幾乎每一刻

28. Nature. 天然、天性、本質、特性

通常是贅字，用法與 character 類似。

* acts of a hostile nature
帶有敵意性質的舉動

hostile acts
不懷好意的舉動

常見於這類語句：「a lover of nature」（愛好自然的人）、「poems about nature」（以大自然為主題的詩歌），語義模糊。除非後面有更明確的陳述，否則讀者無法理解那首詩描寫的是自然風光、田園生活、夕陽、無人踏足過的荒野，還是松鼠的生活習性。

29. Near by. 附近

副詞短語，算不上是優美的英文，雖然和 close by 和 hard by 很相似，似乎行得通。可轉用更好的表達：near 或 near at hand。

切勿用作形容詞，與其意思相近的形容詞為 neighboring。

30. Oftentimes, ofttimes. 通常

這是古用法，現已廢棄。現代的用詞為 often。

31. One hundred and one. 一百零一個

在這個詞組和其他同類詞組中保留 and。這是沿用古英語散文體的表達方式。

32. One of the most. 最……之一

避免在文章開頭或段首用這個詞組，像「One of the most interesting developments of modern science is, etc.」（現代科學其中一個最有趣的發現是……）、「Switzerland is one of the most interesting countries of Europe.」（瑞士是歐洲最令人感興趣的國家之一。）。這樣寫沒有錯，只是予人陳舊老套、言過其實之感。

33. People. 人民

the people 是一個政治用語，不可和 the public 混作一談。人民（the people）會在政治上給予支持或反對；而大眾（the public）則會進行藝術鑒賞或商業贊助。

people 這個字不可以跟數字一起，用來代替 persons。如果六個 people 中走了五個，還有多少個 people 剩下來呢？

34. Phase. 階段

指轉變或發展的階段，如：「the phases of the moon」（月亮的盈虧）、「the last phase」（最後階段）。不可和 aspect（方面）和 topic（話題）混用。

* another phase of the subject
此話題的另一個階段

another point (another question)
另一點（另一個問題）

35. Possess. 擁有

不可僅僅用來替代 have 或 own。

* He possessed great courage.
他擁有非凡的勇氣。

He had great courage (was very brave).
他很有勇氣（很勇敢）。

* He was the fortunate possessor of

他很幸運可以擁有……

He owned

他擁有……

36. Respective, respectively. 各自的（地），個別的（地）

最好略去這些字。

* Works of fiction are listed under the names of their respective authors.

小說類作品根據各作者的姓名列出。

Works of fiction are listed under the names of their authors.

小說類作品根據作者的姓名列出。

* The one mile and two mile runs were won by Jones and Cummings respectively.

一英里和兩英里跑分別由鍾斯和康明斯獲勝。

The one mile and two mile runs were won by Jones and by Cummings.

一英里和兩英里跑由鍾斯和康明斯獲勝。

在一些正式文體裏，例如幾何證明，可能必須使用 respectively，但這個字不應出現在一般主題的寫作中。

37. So. 所以，因此

書寫時避免用 so 來加強語氣，如：「so good」、「so warm」、「so delightful」。

如何用 so 引出從句，請見規則四。

38. Sort of. 有點

參見 kind of。

39. State. 陳述、闡明

不可僅僅用作 say 或 remark 的替代詞。僅用該詞來表示 express fully or clearly（完整清晰地表達），如「He refused to state his objections.」（他不願闡述他的反對意見。）。

40. Student Body. 學生（總稱）

多餘又不順耳，其實意思不過是 students（學生）而已。

*a member of the student body
學生的一員

a student
一個學生

* popular with the student body
受學生歡迎

liked by the students
受學生喜愛

* The student body passed resolutions.
全體學生通過了提案。

The students passed resolutions.
學生們通過了提案。

41. System. 系統、制度

通常是贅字。

* Dayton has adopted the commission system of government.
代頓市採用了委員會管理制度。

Dayton has adopted government by commission.
代頓市接受委員會的管理。

* the dormitory system
宿舍制度

dormitories
宿舍

42. Thanking you in advance. 先行道謝

聽起來作者好像在說：「It will not be worth my while to write to you again.」（不值得我之後再寫信給你了。）。只需要寫上「Thanking you」即可，之後如果你請求的事被允准了，再寫上一封感謝信。

43. They. 他們

一個常犯的錯誤是，在諸如 each、each one、everybody、every one、many a man 這些先行詞之後，用了複數代詞來指代。這類字詞雖然指多於一人，但跟在後面的代詞必須是單數。類似且更不合理的錯誤也見於 anybody、any one、somebody、some one 等，常常有人將這類詞語後面的代詞誤作眾數，其目的可能是想避開引起尷尬的「he or she」這種拗口的表達，或者避免在「he」或「she」中作出選擇。更有羞怯的人會說：「A friend of mine told me that they, etc.」（一位朋友告訴我，他們……）。

除非先行詞確定或必須是女性，否則以上字詞均用 he 指代。

44. Very. 非常、十分

少用這個字。如果真的需要強調，用本身意思強烈的字眼。

45. Viewpoint. 觀點

用 point of view，但切勿和 view、opinion 混用，這種濫用情況很普遍。

46. While. 當

避免胡亂用 while 來取代 and、but 及 although。許多人常用這個字來替代 and 或 but，可能是因為不想連詞千篇一律，也可能是因為不確定這兩個連詞中哪個較恰當。在這種情況下最好用分號取而代之。

這是完全正確的用法，正如以下改寫後的句子所示：

* The office and salesrooms are on the ground floor, while the rest of the building is devoted to manufacturing.
辦公室和賣場在地下，同時其他的樓層都為生產部門所用。

The office and salesrooms are on the ground floor; the rest of the building is devoted to manufacturing.
辦公室和賣場在地下；其他的樓層都為生產部門所用。

如果不會引起混淆或意思不通順，可以在句中表達 although 的意思。

While I admire his energy, I wish it were employed in a better cause.
雖然我欣賞他做事精力充沛，但我真希望他這份精力能運用在更適合的事情上。

I admire his energy; at the same time I wish it were employed in a better cause.

我欣賞他做事精力充沛；同時，我也希望他這份精力能運用在更適合的事情上。

與下列例句比較：

* While the temperature reaches 90 or 95 degrees in the daytime, the nights are often chilly.

Although the temperature reaches 90 or 95 degrees in the daytime, the nights are often chilly.

雖然白天溫度可高達 90 或 95 度，晚上卻通常有點微寒。

改寫成下面的句子後：

The temperature reaches 90 or 95 degrees in the daytime; at the same time the nights are often chilly.

白天溫度可達 90 或 95 度；同時，晚上卻有點微寒。

就可以看出使用 while 來改寫是錯誤的。

一般而言，作者還是使用 while 的字面意思，即 during the time that（在⋯⋯其間）為好。

47. Whom. 誰（關係代詞 who 的賓格）

常在 he said 等短語前被錯誤地用來取代 who。在此處，它實際上是後面動詞的主語。

* His brother, whom he said would send him the money

His brother, who he said would send him the money

他兄弟，也就是他説會寄錢給他的那個人

* The man whom he thought was his friend

The man who (that) he thought was his friend (whom he thought his friend)

他以為是他朋友的那個人

48. Worth while. 值得的

常被濫用，表達含糊的認可或反對（和 not 連用時）。只可以形容或修飾動作，如：「Is it worth while to telegraph?」（這值得發電報嗎？）

* His books are not worth while.

His books are not worth reading (not worth one's while to read; do not repay reading).

他的書不值一讀。

將 worth while 放在名詞前面是不對的，例如「a worth while story」。

49. Would. 將會

第一人稱的條件句用 should，不是 would。

I should not have succeeded without his help.

沒有他的幫忙，我不會成功。

在動詞後面的間接引語中，shall 的過去時態為 should，而不是 would。

He predicted that before long we should have a great surprise.

他預料我們不久會收到一個大驚喜。

表達習慣或重複的動作時，用過去時態往往已足夠，不需要用 would，而且由於語句簡潔，更加有力。

* Once a year he would visit the old mansion.

Once a year he visited the old mansion.

他每年探訪一次舊公寓。

VI

經常拼錯的單字

accidentally
advice
affect
beginning
believe
benefit
challenge
criticize
deceive
definite
describe
despise
develop
disappoint
duel
ecstasy
effect
existence
fiery
formerly
humorous
hypocrisy
immediately
incidentally
latter
led
lose
marriage
mischief
murmur
necessary
occurred
parallel
Philip
playwright
preceding
prejudice
principal
privilege
pursue
repetition
rhyme
rhythm
ridiculous
sacrilegious
seize
separate
shepherd
siege
similar
simile
too
tragedy
tries
undoubtedly
until